WITCH SWINDLED IN WESTERHAM

Paranormal Investigation Bureau Book 2

DIONNE LISTER

Dionne Lister

DEDICATION

This book is dedicated to my first-born, Evan. Love you lots.

CHAPTER 1

I stood in line at Costa and inhaled the rich, sweet aroma of one of my favourite things in the whole world. Coffee. Only two people were before me. Ooh, now it was one.

The blonde woman in front of me with the cute, pink Chanel handbag ordered while her filed-to-points bright-pink nails incessantly tapped the counter: pinky, ring finger, middle finger, pointer finger, repeat. *Tap, tap, tap, tap.* "I'll have a regular coconut-milk latte." Did she realise latte meant milk in Italian? So she's having a coconut-milk milk. The corners of my mouth twitched. Yes, it didn't take much to amuse me.

The young woman behind the counter punched the information into the register. "Would you like any food with that?" Her shoulders tensed, and her smile was tentative.

"If I'd wanted food with that, I would've said. When

have I ever ordered food here? I come in every day and order a beverage. Surely you know what I want by now. And this time, don't burn my coffee." She turned to me and shook her head, speaking loud enough that the whole café could hear. "It's not that complicated, surely? I come in here for a coffee, and I get drama. It would be wonderful if they could employ people with an IQ above one hundred."

Wow. Someone was looking to get their *beverage* spat in. "I'm sure they're doing their best, plus it's probably the boss's orders to ask that question." I risked a smile.

She blinked, her large fake eyelashes slapping together so hard, I almost felt the breeze. An indignant huff was all I got before she turned back around to eyeball the barista. At least the girl behind the register gave me an appreciative smile.

"That'll be two-ninety-five, please." Kudos to her for being polite.

Snarky, rich woman handed over a five-pound note, and when she got her change, counted it… twice. She finally moved out of the way, to wait for her coffee.

"Hi." I smiled. "Can I have a regular skim-milk cappuccino with extra chocolate on top?"

"Sure. And would you like anything to eat?" She grinned, her brown eyes crinkling at the corners.

"I would love something to eat. Thanks for asking." I made sure my perky response was loud enough to reach the area where people were waiting for their orders. "I'll have one of those delicious double-chocolate muffins, thanks."

"Good choice."

She rang it up, and I paid. "Thanks for your awesome service."

"My pleasure. Have a great day!"

"You too." I was still smiling when I stepped over to the waiting area where werewolf-nails stood. I didn't get that claw look. Sure, it might be handy in a dark alley at night, but I'd probably need stitches every time I scratched an itch, and, oh my God, what about wiping after going to the toilet? I shuddered.

She gave me a narrowed side-eyes gaze before jutting her chin up and turning the other way. My work here was done, and I didn't even get stabbed with the shiny, pink talons of death.

Her coffee arrived. She grabbed it and left, taking her negative energy and questionable fashion sense with her.

My coffee arrived, and I found a table near the window. Even though William had given me the coffee maker, I came to Costa every second day. I couldn't resist a cappuccino made by someone else, plus I loved the ambiance here—the warmth, gorgeous food aromas, plus all the British accents floating around.

It had been two weeks since my brother, James's, welcome-home-from-being-kidnapped party, and everything was pretty much back to normal, except that I wasn't going back to Australia. Angelica had magicked herself to the local public toilet at Cronulla Mall—yes, it's gross, but it's a system the witches had set up to have permanent doorways to *travel* to—then walked to my apartment and sent my clothes to my room at her place. She'd slept for two days afterwards—apparently travelling such great distances took a massive amount of a witch's energy. Not all witches could travel over large bodies of water either, which was lucky for James, or I would've been livid that he hadn't visited me for a few years.

I sipped my coffee, then took a bite of the muffin. I savoured the chocolate before washing it down with another mouthful of coffee. Heaven. I smiled to myself, then took my Nikon out of my bag. I'd taken a few photos up and down the high street this morning, and I wanted to look through them. Thankfully, I hadn't picked up on any soon-to-be-dead people or past events. My future-seeing magic only extended to knowing who would die by seeing them through my camera as a ghostly image rather than the solid person they were. Although I hadn't confirmed it yet. It was still an assumption after one ghostly looking person I'd photographed had died soon after. It wasn't a nice feeling knowing that person might soon be dead, and what was I supposed to do with the information? How could you tell a stranger they were going to die soon? And since I didn't know how they would die, what was the point? It's not like I could stop it from happening. Trust me to have some magic that was useless.

Some of the photos were gorgeous. The quaint architecture had me swooning, and the light this morning had been magical. I couldn't wait to get these on my laptop and have a better look.

"Excuse me."

I looked up. It was the girl from behind the register. Her

curly dark hair was in a ponytail, but a tendril had escaped, and she tucked it behind her ear.

I smiled. "Hi."

"Do you have a moment?"

"Yeah, sure."

She sat opposite me. "I'm just on a break, and I wanted to say thanks for before, with that woman. Her name's Camilla. She comes in every day, and she's always rude, but more so with me than anyone else. I can't understand it. I dread the morning shift because of her." She frowned and looked down at her hands in her lap.

"Hey, not a problem. Just happy to help. Some people really suck, but don't let her get you down. She's obviously a bully; call their bluff, and they usually back off. They love an easy target."

She looked up at me. "I'll lose my job if I say anything."

"Surely your boss doesn't want the staff to be harassed. What about workplace health and safety?"

She shrugged.

"What's your name? I'm Lily."

"Hi, Lily. I'm Olivia." She smiled and held out her right hand. I shook it.

"Pleased to meet you."

"Are you from Australia? I love your accent."

"Yes, and thanks." I grinned. "Yours is pretty cool too. I haven't been here long, but it's awesome, so I'm moving here for good. My brother's been here for a few years. He married an English girl."

"Nice." She looked at my camera. "Oh, are you a photographer?"

"Yep. I mainly did weddings and corporate stuff back home, but now I have to start again. I still have my website, but I'm just adjusting it to reflect my recent move. In the meantime, I've been doing the tourist thing and taking photos of the countryside."

She sat up straight and bit her bottom lip. "Do you do engagements?"

"I sure do." Hmm, was this going where I thought it was? I would be so happy to get my first paying job in England. That would be cool.

"Do you have a card? I'm having my engagement party in two weeks, and my cousin was going to take the photos, but he's not a professional. I didn't want to insult him by getting someone else in, but I can say it's payback for you helping me."

I rifled in my bag, skimming my hand through the debris at the bottom. A chewing-gum packet, rogue M&Ms, used tissue, crumpled receipts, and was that sand? Argh, I really needed to clean it out. Phew, there it was. I pulled out a clean, for the most part, card. "Here you go. Check out my website, and if you like my stuff, give me a call. No hard feelings if you decide I'm not right."

She smiled, her eyes shining with excitement. "I'm sure you'll be perfect, but I'll have a look this afternoon." She stood. "I'll give you a call, Lily. And thanks again."

I smiled. "My pleasure. Speak to you soon."

She gave a little wave and returned to her spot behind

the cash register. I finished my muffin and coffee and stood. It was time to return to Angelica's for our daily magic lesson. Some days were theory, but today she was going to teach me how to relocate stuff. Woohoo! Not having to carry the shopping all the way home was going to rock, and what about when I was out and forgot something? No having to dash home or suffer without it.

I left the café, hurried up the hill, and then down our lane. I hadn't tired of the walk yet, and I did it every morning. I'd found a few good routes for jogging, too. When I ran, I soaked in the atmosphere and sights of the pretty town and countryside. Life was good.

Angelica's three-storey Tudor house sat magnificently amidst a formal garden at the front and a cottage garden at the back. A hedge and magnolia trees bordered one side of the driveway, and jasmine covered the tall brick fence behind them—so English.

I let myself in the front door—Angelica actually trusted me to have my own key—it even worked on the reception-room door, although I didn't know how to *travel* yet. I'd had the key for a week and was still surprised I could come and go as I wished. The first week I was here, I was pretty much imprisoned for a lot of it, and after that, everywhere I went, someone chaperoned me, like I was twelve. Although to be fair to my brother, he'd missed me and wanted to spend as much time as we could together while he was on stress leave after being kidnapped. He and his wife, Millicent, were back at work now, so my time was my own.

Hmm, chatting came from the living room. I made my

way to the cosy space. My brother and Angelica sat next to each other on one of the two Chesterfields that faced each other at one end of the room.

"Hi. What are you doing here?"

James smiled. "Hey, Lily. Come sit for a sec."

I sat opposite them on the other Chesterfield and plonked my bag beside me. They both looked at me, assessing. This wasn't promising. "What? Don't look at me like that. Do I have chocolate on my face?" I wiped my hand over my cheeks, mouth, forehead—you could never be too careful. Once I had a big glob of chocolate fudge sauce on my forehead at a friend's wedding, courtesy of a delicious chocolate sundae at the McDonald's drive-through on the way there. I made the entrance of a lifetime to a ballroom full of people. And there I'd been, thinking they were all staring at me because they were floored by my gorgeousness. I should've known better.

Angelica took the lead. "We have a proposition for you."

"Don't say no until you've heard us out." James shuffled forward to the edge of his seat.

"When you put it like that, this sounds like an offer I would love to refuse. What do you want me to do? Clean out the cell toilets at the PIB because, you know, they really could do with a thorough going over. The cells really stink. It's like walking into a men's urinal." They both scrunched their faces in an "ew" expression.

"Too much information, Lily." My brother shook his head.

"Well, you didn't have to spend time there. I did. And it

8

was gross. But as sad as I am for any future incarcerated, I'm not going there again, not even close. The PIB building is dead to me." After being arrested and imprisoned by the Paranormal Investigation Bureau, I swore I'd never set foot in there again, and I meant it. That place scared me.

Angelica and James looked at each other. Great. This *was* something to do with their work at the PIB.

Angelica ran her palms over her skirt, smoothing it. "Sorry, dear, but we need your help on a case. You'd be paid, of course, and I know you haven't gotten any work here yet."

"Well, I might have a job coming up. An engagement party." I sat up straighter and swallowed. I hated saying no to helping them, but I couldn't go back there. "Sorry. I can't. The PIB freaks me out."

James came and sat next to me. "You probably won't have to go anywhere near the Bureau. I need you to take some photos. It's a fraud case. Millions of pounds have been stolen from unsuspecting retirees. We're getting a warrant to search an investment office. The owner's a witch, but her employees and victims are non-witches. We've got witch insiders in the NCA, and they've given this one to us. Once we get enough evidence, we'll prosecute the witch, and they'll handle reporting to the victims, most of who don't even know they've been swindled."

"But what if the witch you're going after has destroyed the evidence? Will it help if we have photos of it and you can't produce the real thing?"

Angelica answered. "The court will accept your

evidence, Lily. There are ways they can test your photos for authenticity. They can tell the difference between real and fabricated evidence, even when it's magic."

James looked at me with his best puppy-dog eyes. "Pleeease. I promise you won't have to go anywhere near the PIB. You're also my favourite sister." He gently shoulder bumped me.

"I'm your only sister." I laughed and engaged sarcastic mode. "Seriously, you're trying too hard. I don't know how I'll hold back saying yes because of your awesome compliment."

"If you won't do it for your favourite brother, at least do it for the old people who've lost their life savings." He tilted his head to the side and pouted.

Argh, he would go and pull that card. Damn him. I took a deep breath. "How much does it pay? Since I'm the only one capable of doing this, I'd imagine it pays well." The money wouldn't hurt. I'd started paying for all the groceries and the Internet because I was home the most. Angelica refused board, since the PIB covered the cost of the house as part of her package, but it wasn't in my nature to freeload, so we'd come to a compromise.

"Fifteen-hundred pounds for each day or part thereof that you're needed," Angelica said.

Say what? Nice. "Okay, then, as long as I don't have to go into the PIB. How many days do you think you'll need me?"

James shrugged. "Could be one, could be five or more. Who knows? It all depends on the evidence you find or don't find in the office. We may need to collect evidence from other locations too."

"You know I can't always see what I want, right?"

Angelica smiled. "Yes, Lily, we know, but we're willing to take that chance. You're our last hope, yet again. You have no idea how valuable your skills are. There's no one else like you in the witch world." Sadness seeped into her eyes. She must be thinking of my mother, who'd been her best friend. I'd inherited my past-and-future seeing abilities from my mum, and she'd been the only witch who could see the past or future before me, but she'd disappeared, most likely murdered, because of what she could do. It meant I was in danger, and now I had two PIB agents following me all the time. My brother made sure I was safe. I didn't like it, but at least the agents stayed hidden most of the time, unless it was his best friends, Beren and William. They tended to keep their distance, but every now and then, they'd say hello.

What was the point of my powers if I couldn't do good with them? Gah. "Okay, I'm in." They both smiled. I didn't share their enthusiasm. "When do you need me?"

James stood. "Now that you've agreed, we can serve the warrant whenever we want. Let me get the squad together, and I'll let you know. Probably this afternoon or tomorrow morning." He turned to Angelica. "You've got lessons with Lily now, don't you?"

"Yes. We're going to concentrate on travelling. She has a bit of work to do before she's ready to do it herself." A bit translated to a crapload. If you made a mistake while building your doorway, you could chop off a toe or end up somewhere you had no idea how to get back from. Not all doorways led to public toilets—somehow that sounded so wrong…. Some bad witches lay traps for other witches. The non-witch world didn't have a monopoly on crazy, sadistic psychopaths. One had to be careful.

"Great. Well, you ladies work on that, and when we're ready to go, I'll come get you both." He waved, mumbled a few words, stepped forward, and disappeared. I shook my head. No matter how many times I saw a witch travelling, I'd never get used to it.

"Ready to learn, Lily?"

"As always. Just don't let me kill myself."

Angelica laughed. "I'll do my best."

CHAPTER 2

After my lesson—which had gone okay, but I still couldn't travel by myself—I'd changed into an official PIB uniform Angelica gave me. I think I looked quite authoritative in my straight-leg black trousers, white shirt, black fitted jacket and black tie, and the cut did wonders for my athletic figure. I had broad shoulders and slightly curvy hips, which suited the PIB getup. I'd pulled my brown hair up into a ponytail and grabbed my camera bag. Since it was an official job, I had three lenses and a spare battery. I'd checked my memory card was wiped and ready to go.

It was 6:00 p.m. Angelica and I sat in her living room while she gave me more background on the case. "We're doing this now because the staff will have left for the day. Fewer hassles that way. The witch under investigation is Camilla Forsyth. We're not positive if she's acting alone or if she has human accomplices. Her staff may be operating under ignorance, but she may have a couple of them in on it. She cons pensioners into giving her their life savings to invest. She invests some of the money, and the rest she just takes. It's not even subtle." Angelica pursed her lips, but I couldn't tell if she was disgusted with what the woman had done or the fact that she didn't do it very well. "Anyway, she's covered her tracks with magic. As far as the regular police are concerned, there's no proof the money ever existed. She's managed to magic away most paper and electronic trails, plus wipe the memories of the pensioners so they have a hard time remembering how much money they had. We've only had one client come forward because out of the blue, he decided to check old bank statements. Memory wiping doesn't work 100 per cent on everyone, especially if you're not an expert. So we need to find out who her clients are as well."

"Why doesn't she just take all their money and run?" That seemed easier to me, but then, I wasn't a criminal mastermind.

"She needs time to follow the trail of money and delete everything that leads to her and the paperwork that proves the money ever existed, so by investing some of the money, she buys herself time before her victims realise what's going on."

"So what am I looking for?"

"Paperwork or images on a screen. We'll concentrate on her desk. If you can get more than one lot of papers or any bank statements, that would be ideal."

"Just getting one would be a good start, considering I'm not very good at this yet."

At least I wouldn't have to photograph any dead bodies or bloody crime scenes. I wasn't sure how I would cope with that, and to be honest, every time I used my camera now, tension knotted my stomach. What if I saw something that gave me nightmares? I figured I had some control, so I always thought of butterflies and chocolate when I used my Nikon—that should keep the bad stuff away.

Gravel crunched outside, accompanied by the quiet rumble of an engine. Angelica and I went out to the drive-way. James sat in the passenger seat of William's Range Rover. I opened the back door. Beren, sexy three-day growth covering his jaw, had a window seat in the back. He grinned, his hazel eyes crinkling at the corners. "If it isn't my favourite Aussie witch. You're rocking the new threads too." He waggled his eyebrows.

I laughed. My cheeks heated. One was never too old to get flustered when a hot man gave them a compliment. "Hey, Beren."

I climbed in and slid across the seat to give Angelica enough room to sit next to me. My thigh touched Beren's as I clicked my seatbelt in, and he pressed his leg against mine. Was that on purpose or because his thick thighs took up a lot of space? My cheeks got hotter. It was a possibility I would spontaneously combust in a minute. I looked up to William's serious grey-eyed gaze in the rear-view mirror. Déjà vu, anyone? He frowned, then changed his focus to the driveway as he reversed to the street.

I took a deep breath and hugged my camera bag closer to my chest. Angelica looked at me. "Are you feeling all right, Lily? You look a little flushed."

Of course she'd notice. "Um, yes. Just nervous about my first assignment."

James cleared his throat. "Is that right?" I didn't even have to see his cheek lifting to know he was smiling—the grin was in his voice.

Oh, crap. I winced. He could tell when someone was lying—his innate talent. Well, it was partly true that I was nervous because of this assignment. Maybe I just had to believe it more. "Yes, that's right." I so wanted to lean over and punch his arm to shut him up before he said something to embarrass me. Hopefully my tone of voice was enough of a message.

"Don't worry, Lily." Beren nudged me with his arm. "This is your second assignment. The proof of how well you did your first assignment is right there." He leaned towards me, reached out and smacked James in the side of the head.

"Hey, ow, man." James rubbed his scalp.

Ha, take that, big brother. "You make an excellent point, B. Thanks." I grinned.

He grinned back. "The pleasure was all mine." No, it wasn't. Trust me.

We weren't in the car for long. William drove to the outskirts of town, to a two-storey brick terrace. We had to park around the corner as there was no street parking. We all got out. James took the lead with William and Beren next, and Angelica stayed beside me. "Got your camera ready?" she asked.

"Yep." I took the lens cap off and jammed it into my pocket, then flicked the camera on.

The sign screwed to the front door said *Camilla Forsyth Investment Solutions*. That name was familiar. Where had I heard it before?

James knocked on the door, a piece of paper in one hand. The door opened.

That's where I knew the name from!

It was Camilla from the café this morning: aka Miss Werewolf-nails. I congratulated myself on being a good judge of character. The fact she was a criminal and didn't earn her Chanel bag fairly wasn't surprising after her performance this morning. She smiled seductively at James before extending it over his shoulder at Beren and William. "Can I help you handsome men?" Her voice was all husky, not at all like the snarkiness from this morning. I kind of felt embarrassed for her. Wait till she found out they weren't here to ask her on a date. Would it be rude of me to get some photos of the moment?

"Are you Camilla Forsyth, investment broker?"

She put her palm to her chest, showing off her talons. "Why, yes, I am. What can I do for you? Are you looking to invest?" Wow, she was even willing to rip off these guys. Either she was really good at magicking away the evidence or she wasn't nearly as smart as Angelica gave her credit for.

"Are any of your employees still here?"

She furrowed her forehead. "No, why?"

James held up the warrant. "I have a warrant to search your premises. We're from the Paranormal Investigation Bureau. Please step aside."

Her smile faltered. "What? Where? The Paranormal what?" Was she playing dumb, or did some witches not know about the PIB?

"Don't play stupid with me, Miss Forsyth. If you don't let us in, one of my colleagues will arrest you for obstructing an investigation." There was my answer.

William held up his cuffs and jangled them. I shuddered. I'd had my fill of handcuffs for the rest of my life.

Camilla folded her arms. "What's this about?"

"You're under investigation for fraud. This is your last chance to step out of the way, Miss Forsyth." Wow, my brother was tough when he wanted to be.

She snatched the warrant papers and stalked back into the building, leaving the door open for the rest of us to enter. The guys hurried through the reception area and fanned out. There was much stomping and doors opening and closing. It sounded like kids running riot, but without the laughing and screaming.

"Wait here, Lily." Angelica left me in the front reception room and followed James further into the house. Should I start taking photos or should I wait to be asked? We didn't have all night. May as well start now.

Footsteps clacked on the timber floor. "I thought I recognised you." Camilla planted her feet shoulder-width apart and folded her arms, the paperwork dangling from one hand. "Were you following me?"

So, maybe I wouldn't be starting those photos just yet. No matter, I was sure I could annoy her while I waited for Angelica to return. "No. I was having coffee, and a chocolate muffin, which was delish, by the way. You should try one some time. They're totally worth a little extra booty."

"Booty? Why are you using that word? You don't sound American."

"I'm not, but I like the word. Booty, booty, booty." I smiled. She didn't. "Booty." Hmm, still nothing. Meh, she was no fun. "Is this where your receptionist sits?" I pointed to the lime-washed timber desk, which had normal office paraphernalia neatly organised on it.

"What do you think?"

I could tell her what I thought, about her in particular, but I'd probably get into trouble from Angelica. I had to be professional. Maybe I should've thought of that before taunting her with my booty. I snorted. I really was funny; it was a shame she didn't appreciate me. Her lips pursed.

"I'll take that as a yes. Thanks." I brought my camera to my face and studied the desk through the viewfinder.

"What are you doing? There's nothing in here about taking photos." She shook the papers above her head, just in case I didn't notice them. Dramatic much?

Another set of shoes clomped in. "It's in the fine print. Part of normal procedure, Miss Forsyth." Angelica to the rescue. She handed me a pair of rubber gloves. "Put these on. Start with that desk, Lily, and don't be afraid to open drawers."

"Yes, Ma'am." I slipped the gloves on and got to work

by focusing my thoughts on investment paperwork. Hopefully that would be enough. A yellow manila folder appeared on the desk, but it was closed. I walked around the other side of the desk and took a picture of it right-side up. *O'Connell 2017/18* was written neatly in black marker on the front. I opened all three drawers and looked inside. Staples, pens, pencils, highlighters, Post-its. Nothing out of the ordinary.

I lowered the camera. "Which room next?"

"We'll start with her associate's office. He's not a witch, but from what we know, he's invested some of the money from those who've been swindled." Angelica gave Camilla an I'm-coming-for-you glare, then turned and led me to an office off the hallway. The click, click, click of Camilla's heels echoed as she followed closely. She must be crapping herself. Was it bad that this brought happiness to my heart? I really needed to work on my empathy. Maybe I'd start tomorrow.

Baby-blue walls radiated calm. A red leather office chair sat on one side of the shiny-topped walnut table, and two dark blue chairs sat on the other. A little golden plaque on the table, facing the guest chairs, read *Ernest Smythe*. So, that was our other suspect, the non-witch one.

I wondered if he knew she was a witch. Had she coerced him with the promise of the normal stuff—money, sex, or blackmail—or did she trap him in a spell? She could even have planted thoughts in his head. Apparently my brother could do that—talk people into stuff they didn't want to do —but it wasn't his style. It wasn't something witches were allowed to do, either. If he was caught doing it, even to help solve a crime, he could go to jail. Not to mention, most witches had a spell to counteract mind coercion. Except, I didn't. My eyes widened. I'd have to learn that one as soon as possible. Just in case.

Camilla pushed past me and stood in front of the desk. "There's nothing here. You're wasting your time."

Angelica walked to the filing cabinet and opened the first drawer. "Then why are you so worried?"

"I'm not. I'm very good at what I do." Camilla folded her arms and turned to watch Angelica, who was pulling folders out. There actually weren't that many. Seemed Camilla might be right, but she didn't know about my skills.

I went to the other side of the desk and looked through my camera. *Who have you ripped off? Show me the files.* I listened for the hum of power that witches had access to. It filled my head, slid over my body, and I breathed it in, immersed myself in the warm, slightly prickly sensation. Two open files appeared on the table. I wasn't going to waste time reading the whole thing, but there were three pages laid out. I clicked away.

"Why are you photographing an empty desk?"

I finished what I was doing and looked at Camilla. "It's a potential crime scene. Isn't that obvious?" I wore my most innocent expression. I knew she had no idea of what I could do, but it was fun messing with her. Plus, Angelica wanted my secret skills to remain as secret as possible. There was no sense telling all the criminals I could spy on what they'd done in the past. I was sure the price on my head would go up if everyone knew. Crap. I hadn't thought of that before.

It was bad enough having my parents' enemies after me; now I had to worry about everywitch else.

Angelica looked at me. "Are you okay, dear?"

"Um, yeah. I just can't remember if I switched the iron off this morning."

She gave me a weird look. Probably because she'd given me my clothes crease free. Being a witch, she probably didn't even own an iron. Surely there was a spell for dewrinkling clothes.

Camilla laughed. "You call yourself a witch, and you still use a conventional iron like a plain old human?"

I shrugged. "I like to keep things real." Tuning everyone out, I opened the bottom desk drawer first. Paperwork would most likely be there since all the stuff you needed daily should be the easiest to access, i.e. in the top drawer. There were a few files. I took them out for Angelica to go over later; then I used my camera on the "empty" drawer. A pile of files appeared, but I could only read the title on the first manila folder: McMaster 2015/16. *Click.* Seemed this racket had been going on for a while. I wondered when Camilla had started buying Chanel handbags and having her nails talonified? The PIB was probably all over her bank accounts and spending habits. That's probably part of how they'd come to this point.

The next two drawers had nothing of relevance, so I stood against the wall behind the desk and pointed my camera at the room.

"I didn't give you permission to photograph me." Camilla glared at me.

"Well, get out of the way, then. Go bother the guys. I'm sure they're doing way more interesting stuff." I wondered if they'd found anything.

She spun and strode out. The atmosphere in the room relaxed noticeably. Angelica rustled through the filing cabinet while I focussed on my job. I whispered, "Show me the relationship between Camilla and Mr. Smythe." The two of them popped into his chair, and I stepped back and slammed into the wall. Doh! Would I ever get used to these images popping in and out? It was disconcerting, because it was in 3D, like they were really there, albeit frozen in time.

I walked to the other side of the desk so I could see them from the front. He looked to be in his late twenties, a couple of years younger than her. His dark hair was slicked back with some kind of product—it looked oily, to be honest. Not my thing. They were both fully clothed, thank God, but his red tie was on the desk and his three top shirt buttons undone. She had her hand against his bare chest. Her face was tilted up to his. Her eyes were closed, their lips almost touching. So it *was* sex. He looked pretty into it, with his hand on her boob, so I didn't think blackmail was going to factor into it.

Click. Click.

I lowered the camera and shut my eyes, kind of resetting myself. When I opened my eyes, they were gone. Thank God for small mercies. I went around to the other side again and concentrated on the desk. An open laptop appeared, Mr. Smythe sitting in his chair staring at the screen, his hands poised above the keyboard. A bank webpage was open on the screen. *Click.* I shut my eyes, willed the information to change, and opened my eyes again. A new page appeared on the screen, and Smythe wore a white shirt instead of the blue one he had on just a moment ago. Wow, this was cool, except maybe I'd be here all day now. Yikes.

After getting six different web pages to appear, the images stopped coming. I looked up. Angelica watched me with a carefully blank expression. I hardly ever knew what was going on in her head—she was the master of concealing her thoughts.

"I'm done."

"Did you see anything?"

"Yes, but I don't want to talk about it here."

"Good idea. Let's move to the next office then." She started for the door.

It was going to be a long afternoon.

Three hours later, we walked out the door, which Camilla slammed behind us, the noise echoing down the street. Someone was cranky, and it couldn't have happened to a nicer person.

It'd possibly been a fruitful search, if the number of photos I'd taken were anything to go by. I didn't know if what I'd captured was criminal stuff or normal, but we'd soon find out. Well, the PIB would. I wasn't sure if I was going to be privy to that information.

We weren't actually far from home. It would take me maybe ten minutes to walk. I took the memory card out of my camera and handed it to Angelica. "Take this. I'm going to walk home." I'd gone for a run that morning, but I felt like some fresh air after being in that building all evening. It was still light enough to see—the sun went down late over here in late spring and summer. Even in the middle of summer in Sydney, our sunsets happened around eight or eight thirty.

"I don't want you walking home alone at this time of night," James said.

I clenched my jaw. I'd taken care of myself for far too long for him to be trying to manage my life now. "I'm a little bit too old for you to boss around. I'd like some fresh air."

James stood closer and spoke quietly. "You're not safe, Lily. Please don't give me extra stuff to worry about."

"What other stuff do you have to worry about? I would've thought work was old news by now."

"Something I can't discuss right now. Nothing bad, per se, but I've got a lot on my plate. Please, Lily?"

I sighed. Guilt sucked. "Okay."

Beren looked at James. "I'd be happy to walk her home, if that's okay with you? And Thompson and Bourke are on tailing detail tonight. She'll be perfectly safe."

James narrowed his eyes at his friend, and William scowled. "Jesus, guys. He's walking me home. We'll be fine. What am I, seven?"

William turned and stalked towards the car. James sighed. "No, but you're still my little sister. Beren, if anything happens to her…"

Beren clapped him on the shoulder. "I'll protect her with my life."

That seemed to satisfy James. "Be careful."

"We will." I gave him a quick hug. "See you later. Say hi to Mill for me."

"Will do." He turned and followed William.

Angelica smiled. "He'll always be your big brother, Lily. I know it's hard, but try and go easy on him. He's had a tough time since your parents disappeared."

The sadness I tried to ignore flared, singeing my heart. "I know, but I'm not helpless. God knows I survived by myself in Sydney all the years he's been here. I don't need a parent anymore. Maybe I'm old enough to just need a brother. I'll see you later. Are you going to be home tonight?"

"Probably after midnight. Beren, maybe you could have dinner with Lily before you come back into headquarters?"

"It would be my pleasure." He looked at me and smiled. "Let's go."

Well, if I had to have a babysitter, it may as well be a tall, attractive man who made me laugh. As we walked home, chatting and laughing, I couldn't help thinking I wished William had volunteered to take me home. I knew I was an idiot, so I mentally slapped myself across the face. Not that anything would happen with either of these guys. There's no way dating any of my brother's friends was a good idea, and I was sure they'd agree.

Once we got home, I checked out the fridge. "How do you feel about leftover spaghetti bolognaise? I can make a salad to go with it."

"Sounds good to me. I love anything I don't have to cook myself."

"I'd say you're such a guy, but James is a good cook. He and Millicent share cooking duties fifty-fifty."

"Ah, yes, but James is awesome."

"Hard to argue with that." I smiled and got the lettuce, tomatoes, and cucumbers out of the fridge, then put the spaghetti in the microwave to reheat. While I made the salad, Beren set the table... with a spell. Angelica's plates, knives, forks, and napkins appeared out of nowhere. "Someone's going to have to teach me that some day."

"Isn't Angelica teaching you?"

"Yes, but we haven't covered transporting things yet. We're still working on travelling." The microwave dinged. Before I could get the spaghetti out, it appeared in the middle of the table. "Show off." I laughed and sat at the table. Beren joined me, and we spooned food onto our plates. "Which side of your family does your magic come from?"

"Both. That's why my magic is strong, same with William. When one parent is human, it can dilute the power —not all the time but in most cases. You and James are exceptions, probably because the magic is strong on your mother's side."

"But I thought witches couldn't tell humans they existed?"

"They can't, but if you fall in love with a non-witch, you can tell them if they agree to a kill spell."

"The type stupid Snezana asked me to agree to?"

"Exactly."

"Wow, that's harsh."

"It goes for friends too."

"But what if your friend or partner accidentally tells a non-witch when they're drunk or something?"

Beren shrugged. "Bad luck, I suppose. That's why it's best to stick to other witches when it comes to having friends and falling in love." Was it my imagination or was he looking at me more intently? Knowing me, I was reading more into things than were there.

"What about you and William? Do you guys date; are you married? Um, not to each other. Oh my God. I mean, you know, in general. Although, it would be fine if you were together." I snort-laughed. *Way to go, Lily.*

He laughed, and a bit of spaghetti flew out of his mouth and landed on the table. "Um, no. No way. He's handsome and all, but he's a bit grumpy for my taste. Plus, he's had his heart broken, poor man, so he's sworn off any relationship longer than a week. But seriously, the job takes up so much time that it's hard to date. We obviously, you know, *meet* women sometimes. Short relationships mean non-witches aren't off limits. You don't have to explain much when it's not serious. James and Millicent have lasted because they work together. They *get* the job and what it involves."

"But what if you fell in love by accident? It can happen, you know." It'd never happened to me, but I'd seen it happen to friends, and when it ended, all hell broke loose.

"I know what I like." There was that intense hazel-eyed gaze again. "If I fall in love, it won't be by accident."

Oh my. Was it hot in here? I resisted the urge to fan myself with my hand because that would have looked so dumb. Surely he didn't like me like that. Did he? Not that I'd be against it, but it would be awkward with James, especially when we broke up. Man, I was crazy. We weren't even close to dating, and I'd already envisaged the end of the non-existent relationship. *Whoa there, Lily.*

I changed the subject so I could finish my meal without *assuming* myself into spontaneously combusting.

After dinner, Beren magicked everything into the dishwasher. Score! "Thanks for dinner, Lily. I really enjoyed the food and the company." He smiled.

"Me too."

He leaned down and hugged me. Admittedly, my stomach did have a few butterflies while I was wrapped in his strong, warm arms, but it was best to pretend I didn't enjoy it because nothing good could come from dating Beren... or William. Gah. William wasn't here. I did not need to be thinking about him. I was starting to bore myself with my stupidity.

"Night, Lily." He stood back and waved.

"Night."

And just like that, he was gone.

CHAPTER 3

The cold air burned my throat. I jogged through the cool morning, enjoying the tunes on my iPhone. Music was an awesome way to lessen the ache in my legs in the final kilometre of my eight-kilometre run. I looked behind me and waved.

This morning Beren and William were on protect-Lily detail. They diligently kept fifty-metres behind me. Why didn't they just run with me? It wasn't like I didn't know they were there. I felt like some important or famous person, but I didn't have any of the cool things that went with it, like money, adoring fans, and the free stuff. Why did rich people get free stuff all the time? That just bugged me. They could afford to pay for it, for God's sake. Yeah, I knew it was potential advertising to have your products seen on a famous person, but still, how did they live with themselves? Greedy bastards. I felt bad if someone tried to buy me a three-dollar coffee.

The phone rang, cutting off my tunes. My earphones had a microphone, so I pressed answer. "Hello, Lily speaking," I panted.

"Are you okay? Have I got you at a bad time?"

"No, just going for my morning run. Who's this?"

"Oh, sorry. It's Olivia. Um, I've had a look at your website, and I love your style. I was wondering if you'd be available to photograph my engagement party?"

Oh, that was a surprise. Yay! My first proper job. Yesterday didn't count, since my brother technically got the job for me, and they hadn't wanted me for my creative skills. "I'd love to! Just text me where and when, and I'll be there. Also"—this was always the most awkward part of the conversation for me, which was stupid because no one, except for famous rich people, expected stuff for free—"I require 20-per cent payment upfront and the rest just before I send your edited photos. If you fill in the online form and tick the package you're after, that would be great."

"For sure. I'll do that this morning. Thanks! I'm so excited, but, aye, a lot of planning goes into engagements. Now I'm scared to delve into the wedding planning, because it's going to be so much worse."

"Elope." I laughed and puffed at the same time.

"Ha, yeah. You never know. It may just come to that. Are you going to be in later today?"

"To Costa?"

"Yes."

"Yep."

"I'll see you later, then. Bye."

"Bye."

My driveway was in sight, so I sprinted the last hundred metres. My throat burned as I dragged as much air into my lungs as possible. I reached the driveway and stopped, then bent at the waist, resting my hands on my thighs. Exercise was invigorating and set me up for the rest of the day, but, man, did it hurt. Sometimes I questioned my sanity.

The crunch of Beren and William's sneakers on the gravel came from behind me. I straightened, moving my hands to my waist. "Morning."

Beren grinned. William gave me a chin tip but no smile. Really? Was that how he greeted everyone, or did he especially hate me? "Have you got a stone in your shoe, William?"

His forehead scrunched in cute confusion. "Huh? No."

"Why the cranky face then? Are you pissed you have to follow me all over the place? It wouldn't hurt you to smile once in a while."

Beren looked at his watch. "Hey, Lily! You ran a good time this morning. You've shaved a minute off last time. You set a pretty good pace."

Way to change the subject. Argh. For Beren's sake, I'd drop it. "I try. I'm sure you guys weren't pushing too hard, though."

Beren shrugged. "Maybe not as hard as we could, but it wasn't a walk in the park."

"You may want to get showered and changed. I'm going

to the café this morning. See you in the distance later." I gave them a huge, exaggerated smile—yeah, I couldn't help myself, always poking the bear—then went inside.

After showering, I dressed in jeans, T-shirt, jumper and hiking boots—it may be late spring, but it was still cold. Top temp today was going to be sixteen Celsius. That was like winter in Sydney. Instead of my camera, I put one of Mum's diaries into my handbag—the last one she'd finished before she disappeared. I'd read them all, but I was more interested in the recent ones. If what James said was true, and there were clues hidden in the pages, I wanted to start with the stuff that happened in the UK, since I could look into it here.

In the downstairs hallway, I ran into Angelica, who was just coming out of the reception room. "Good morning, Lily. How was your run?"

"Great, thanks. I'll never tire of the countryside. I love Westerham."

She smiled. "I'm so glad you're settling in. I have to go back to work soon, but I wanted to thank you again for yesterday. Many of the photos you took had some of what we needed. We've been able to identify five more of the clients she's stolen from. And a couple of the screenshots and the paperwork from that file are going to help immensely in court, although we're not really any closer to arresting Camilla. She's been careful to make it look like it's all her associate. She'll plead ignorance and get a slap on the wrist if we take action now. Also, we need to know if her accomplice is a willing and knowing participant, or if she's spelled him into it. Anyway, I just wanted you to know that you really have a valuable skill. Your mother would have been proud."

Pride and melancholy filled my heart to aching. What I wouldn't give to have my mother here now. I sighed and gave Angelica a sad smile. "Thanks. I'm glad to hear I got something you could use, even if Camilla's still in the clear."

"I'm going back now, but enjoy your day, dear, and stay out of trouble."

"Yes, Ma'am."

Angelica stepped forward and disappeared. She must be good. Most witches I'd seen performing spells had to say something first. She must have it down to a fine art.

It didn't take long to walk to Costa, and the grey sky kindly kept its moisture to itself. A warm blast of air impregnated with the rich scents of coffee and cake whooshed into my face when I opened the door. Ahhhh. My happy place.

Groundhog Day anyone? Camilla was ordering in her usual shitty way. "Don't burn my coffee. And this change is sticky. Give me new change."

I snorted. The things some people did for attention. *Oops, I think she heard me.* She turned and scowled. Her dilated pupils were filled with a whirlpool of anger that I swear was trying to suck me in and disappear me forever. I couldn't feel any tingles of power, so I should be safe. It was almost as if she was daring me to say something.

"Morning." I waggled my fingers in a silly wave.

She growled, turned back to Olivia, and held out her

hand for different change. Olivia obliged, then looked at me. "Next!"

I grinned. "My usual, thanks."

"Regular skim cap with extra chocolate and a double-chocolate muffin coming right up."

I handed her the right money because I was an old hand at this now.

She leaned forward and spoke quietly. "I might take my break soon and join you for five minutes. Is that okay?"

"Yeah, sure. We can chat all things engagement party."

She rolled her eyes, but her grin told a different story. Ah, young love.

Camilla ignored me while we waited, which was fine with me. Soon after she left, my order was done, and I was sitting at my favourite table by the front window. I slid my mum's diary out of my bag and started on page one for the second time. I'd gone on a reading binge in order to finish all the diaries, but I'd been so eager to read through them that I'd already forgotten most of what was in there. Now it was time to comb through them and see if I could find any clues. There was still the chance James was wrong, but my mum was smart, and it totally sounded like something she would think of doing.

This diary started 1ˢᵗ January, 2007. Each diary had a couple of years in it, as she didn't write in it every day. Maybe that was a hint in itself? Or maybe some were things she just wanted to remember, and others were days with clues? I guessed if you were trying to hide a needle in a haystack, you needed a lot of straw. It wouldn't do to be too obvious.

Mum's neat black cursive, with loopy, angled script, covered the page. Her neatness was something I hadn't inherited. My writing was so messy; even I couldn't decipher it most of the time. I may as well trust my memory for all the good my writing was, and that's saying something.

Enjoyed last night, New Year's Eve, with the kids and Joe on holidays at the beach. I can't believe another year's gone so fast. What will this year bring? James and Lily are growing so fast. I know one day we won't have these family holidays, so I'm enjoying it while I can. Lily collected seashells today, and we're going to wash them and make something. I'm not sure what, but whatever it is, I hope I still have it in years to come, as a reminder of this wonderful time. And I hope Lily always has it and knows part of me is there with her. Is it wrong to be sad that the kids have to grow and leave? Being a parent is so bittersweet. Well, that's it for today. Over and out. K.

I blinked away the burn in my eyes. I remembered that holiday, and we had made something out of the shells. We'd stuck them onto a couple of small picture frames—one sat on Mum's dressing table, and one sat on mine, until she never came home. Now I had them both, but they were in one of four boxes I'd kept when I'd moved. They were still in my garage at home. I wondered if Angelica could go and grab them for me. Or maybe I could ask James. Not that I thought there were clues in them. At the moment, the memories were more important.

"Hey, Lily."

I shut the diary and looked up. "Hey, Olivia. Break time?"

She nodded and sat. "I filled in the form on your site today. I picked package two, and I've paid the deposit."

"Awesome. I haven't checked my emails today. What date is the party?"

"Not this Saturday, but the next. We're having it at my parents'. It's an afternoon thing."

"I'll definitely be there. I know the planning sucks, but are you excited?"

She grinned. "Totally. We've been dating for two years, and I can't wait to get married. It feels right, you know?"

I nodded, even if I didn't really know. I'd been attracted to few men, dated some, but I couldn't say I'd ever been in love. "What's he like? Is he older than you?"

"He's five years older. Twenty-eight. Just a warning: he and my dad don't get along too well. My dad puts up with him, but he says he isn't good enough for me. Typical dad, huh?"

Something else I wouldn't know. Gah. I pushed away the sad and held onto the happy. This was a massive thing for her, and she should enjoy it as much as possible. "I'm sure your dad's only like that because he loves you. He'll probably come around once you're married."

"I hope so." She twisted a loose strand of curly hair around her finger. "Hey, you're fairly new in town, so you probably don't know a lot of people. Ernie and I are going to the wine bar, No. 17, on Friday night with a few friends. Would you like to come?"

I wasn't a super social person, but I was in a new place, and I should be trying new things. Plus, Olivia seemed really nice. "Yeah, sure. What time?"

"Seven. That's when everyone who works in London usually gets back."

"Does your fiancé work in London?"

"No. He used to, but he started working locally a couple of years ago. Just around the time we met, actually. A few of his mates still work up there. Anyway, I'd better get back to it. Thanks again, and I'll see you tomorrow night."

"For sure. Thanks for the invite." I smiled. She waved and made her way back to her register.

I finished my food and coffee and decided to go home. Reading my mum's diary had taken the bouncy happy out of my day, and I had washing to do. I inhaled a quick breath. Yikes, tomorrow night was Friday night, and I didn't like wine. Crap. Why had I agreed to go? *And*, I only had thirty hours or so to figure out what to wear.

As I walked home, I hoped they had Baileys Irish Cream at this wine bar. I think it must be the same one I'd visited on my first day. At least it had a cosy ambiance, and hopefully her friends would be good company. You never knew when you would meet someone who turned out to be a best friend. And if I wasn't having fun, I could say I had a headache and walk home, since it wasn't far.

I held onto that thought as I went inside and started the washing.

THE NEXT NIGHT, AT SIX FORTY-FIVE, I STOOD IN FRONT OF the mirror in skinny black jeans, high-heeled knee-length black boots, and a semi-tight red polo neck jumper. The rest of my clothes lay strewn on my bed, so I couldn't even see the covers. It had only taken five outfit changes to find one I was comfortable with. I even had make-up on and my straight hair down. What was the world coming to? I couldn't remember the last time I'd dressed up, and yes, jeans was still dressing up, at least for me. I wasn't averse to showing a bit of cleavage either, but it was too damn cold for that. My girls wanted to stay warm, and I was only too happy to oblige them.

I grabbed my clutch and teetered downstairs. I wasn't bad in heels, but I didn't wear them much, so I wasn't the most elegant in them. I didn't know how supermodels did it, gliding down the runway and in awkward clothes to boot. I guess that's why they earned the big bucks. Okay, so it wasn't a valuable skill, but whatever.

As I clopped across the hallway floor, Angelica came out of the living room.

"Hi, Ma'am. I didn't know you were home."

"I got back about ten minutes ago. Are you off to the wine bar again?" She smirked.

I sniffed. I'd had a perfectly good and non-alcoholic reason for being there the first and only time I'd been, but she'd made a big deal about me drinking in the morning. "Yep."

"Are you walking?"

"I thought I might. It's still light out, although I'm not

sure how I'll go in these boots." Maybe I should change them.

"It's too late for that, dear. You're going to be late."

Crap. I'd forgotten to shield my thoughts. Angelica was a mind reader extraordinaire, and I should know better.

"Yes, you should." She tittered; she was too cultured to giggle.

"Doesn't take much to make you laugh," I grumbled. I already felt stupid. There was no need to rub my witchy face in it. I said the words to shield my thoughts. *Done. And stay out.*

"Would you like a lift to the wine bar?"

"I won't say no. Only if it's not too much trouble."

"Of course not, dear." Angelica pulled out her phone and pressed a couple of buttons. "Are you boys close by? Good. Can you give Lily a lift up to the wine bar? Yes… She's going out tonight." She rolled her eyes. "I don't know. Ask her yourself. See you soon." She hung up and turned to me. "That's the most I've heard William say in a while. He doesn't seem to like the idea of you going out. Anyway, dear, you can wait outside. They'll be here in a jiffy. Have fun."

I half laughed. Trust her to offer for someone else to give me a lift. "I will. Thanks, Ma'am." Great, Agent Crankypants was going to be in fine form. At least it was only a two-minute drive.

As soon as I'd shut the front door, William's black Range Rover turned into the driveway. He pulled up next to me, and I got into the back seat. "Hey."

"Big night planned?" asked Beren.

No, but they didn't have to know that. "My new friend from Costa asked me out with her and her friends. I'm looking forward to having a few beverages and kicking back. It's been a while since I've had any fun. I just hope I don't drink too much and vomit." I giggled because I was sure that made me sound even more clueless.

William didn't just scowl at me through the mirror, as per usual. He actually turned around, lifted his pointer finger, and aimed it at me. His angry face was firmly in place. "Be careful. It's not safe for a single woman out there alone. Don't leave your drink unattended. Don't go home with any strangers, and don't drink too much. If anything happens to you, James will have our heads. So don't be stupid, Lily. Got it?"

I rolled my eyes—both for effect and because he was being overly dramatic. "What. Do I have two fathers now? You and James need to settle, petal. I'm twenty-four, not twelve, and I can go out and have fun with my new friends. It's not up to you to say what I do or don't do, and you can pass that onto James if he has a problem with it." Honestly, did anyone ever tell the guys what they could and couldn't do? Besides, I wasn't an idiot. He glared harder, if that were even possible.

Beren shook his head, but his tone was softer. "Please just look after yourself, Lily. We'd hate if anything happened to you. Okay?"

Argh! How could I be snarky when he was so nice? "Don't worry. I was kidding about the drinking too much. I don't even like wine. Look, I'll be careful. Besides, you guys'll be outside lurking somewhere. Why don't I call you when I'm ready to go home, and you can give me a lift?"

William's jaw unclenched, and his shoulders relaxed a little, but the grooves in his forehead stayed firmly embedded.

Beren said, "Thank you."

"No problem." I huffed out a breath and looked out the window. It was nice to have people who cared, but I was feeling a bit smothered. And it wasn't like they cared about me because they liked *me* in particular. They felt a sense of duty to my brother, so it was like having three brothers, or two dads and a brother. I had to admit that Beren wasn't as painful to deal with as William or James. Even Angelica seemed okay with me going out. It was probably because she was a woman, and she understood how it felt to be unnecessarily overprotected.

I breathed deeply, then let my frustration go. I was going to have fun tonight, whether William and Beren wanted me to or not. *So there.* I stuck my tongue out at the back of William's seat.

"Very mature, Lily. You know I can see you." William raised his brows at me in the rear-view mirror, but I saw his lips twitch.

"Good." I grinned.

He shook his head. "We're here." William pulled up to the kerb. That really was quick. I should've walked.

"Thanks for the lift. I'll give you a call later. You'll still be on duty at 4:00 a.m., won't you?"

William opened his mouth, no doubt to lecture, but

Beren laughed, cutting him off. "Good one, Lily. If you're not out by the time we get off at one, we'll just carry you out."

My mouth dropped open. "You wouldn't!"

Beren grinned. "Yes, we would. Now go have fun, and stay out of trouble."

Argh! Living here was never going to work. Maybe I should move back to Australia. I slid out of the car into the bright sunlight. "See ya." I didn't know if I would ever get used to it being light until after 7:00 p.m. in spring. It did feel so much safer because of that. There were no shadows to hide in. But I really should learn some attacking spells. There must be a witch Taser-type spell. If there wasn't, I was totally going to invent it.

I crossed the road to the pretty Tudor building I'd visited on my first day in Westerham. This time when I pushed the door open, it was to the sound of excited chatter, laughing, jazz music through speakers, and lots of people. Many of them were in work clothes: shirts, jackets, black or grey skirts and pants. I was glad I'd worn jeans—a dress would've been a bit much, not that I had a lot of dresses. I'd always been a bit of a tomboy, tagging along with James and his friends, even though I knew they hated having me around. I was always James's annoying little sister, until our parents disappeared. That was when he became more protective, and he preferred having me where he could keep an eye on me.

There were so many people that it took me a minute to find Olivia. There she was, sitting at a table in the corner.

She saw me and waved. I waved back and headed over. She was sitting with seven others.

Oh my God. My eyes widened, but then I quickly tried to look as normal as possible. My heart raced. This wasn't going to be good. How was I supposed to fake it all night? It was time to channel Angelica's poker face.

"Hey, Lily. I'm so glad you could make it!" Olivia stood and gave me a hug. "This is my fiancé, Ernie." She beamed, and he held out his hand to shake mine.

This could not be happening. I held out my hand and hoped my smile came across as legit and not crazy town. "Lovely to meet you, Ernie." But it wasn't lovely to meet him. I resisted the urge to crush his hand in mine.

"Lovely to meet you too, Lily. I hear you're going to be our official photographer next weekend." Ernie was Ernest Smythe, the man with the slicked-back hair who I'd seen through my camera making out with none other than Olivia's archenemy, Camilla.

I'd had a feeling I shouldn't have come. When would I learn to trust my instincts?

I sat. This was going to be a long night.

CHAPTER 4

M uch to William and Beren's satisfaction, I called them at eleven thirty. Olivia's friends were nice, and she was a lot of fun, but all I could think about was that her fiancé was cheating on her and what the hell was I supposed to do? Not to mention I might have a hand in getting her fiancé arrested for ripping people off. I opened my mouth about four times to tell Olivia what I knew. It had been a massive struggle to keep the information to myself. What kind of friend did that make me?

I was quiet the entire ride home: all of two minutes.

"Is something wrong?" Beren asked when we reached Angelica's.

There was no point telling them anything, yet. I needed to work things out in my head first. I knew that once they knew, it would be up to me to get some covert information on him, and I still had to photograph their engagement, unless he was arrested first. And what would happen to my new friendship with Olivia when she finally found out I'd helped put her man in jail? I crossed my fingers that he was an unwilling participant. Yeah, right.

"No. It was really noisy, and it's been a while since I've been out. Maybe I miss my friends a little too. But I'm fine." That was the truth. I'd been away for almost two months, and I'd never gone that long without seeing my friends. I messaged them every now and then, but since we were in opposite time zones, I hadn't had a chance to call. And I hadn't told them I was moving for good yet. Even though my paperwork was in, it didn't mean I wouldn't change my mind.

"You didn't leave early because of us, did you?" William had turned around, and those wrinkles were back on his forehead. He was going to age prematurely if he kept that up.

"No. Don't flatter yourself." I laughed, taking the sting out my words. "I had fun. Shout-talking isn't my favourite thing. Olivia and I have arranged to go into London next week sometime. I've never been, and there's so much to see. She offered to show me around." I was really looking forward to it, too. Maybe I'd check Mum's diary and see if she and Dad had done anything in London. They'd been a few times since I was born. It must have been for PIB stuff, now that I think about it. Maybe they contracted Mum to work sometimes, like they were doing with me now. I'd have to ask Angelica. "Night."

"Night," they said at the same time.

I went inside and straight to the freezer. Tonight called for ice cream. I opened the freezer door. *Bummer. Nothing.* I pouted. Frozen peas, ice cubes, frozen chicken, and that was it. Angelica probably didn't eat ice cream. In fact, I'd never seen her do anything for fun. I'd have to rectify that. Everyone needed some soul-feeding time—and I didn't just mean food. Doing your favourite thing was good for your mental health. Photography and running were it for me. Nothing could cheer me up like a good bout of exercise or ice cream, okay, and coffee. I sighed. But there was no ice cream. *Whaaaaa!* I wished I knew more magic. Then I'd travel myself to the nearest supermarket via the public toilet, grab some chocolate-choc-chip extravaganza and pop back.

Beaten on all fronts, I trudged up to my room. There was nothing left to do but go to sleep. I turned on the light. Argh! My bed was a garbage dump of clothes. Okay, so they were clean clothes, but I didn't want to put them all away now. My shoulders slumped.

"Lily. You're home early."

I turned. Angelica was in a fluffy white dressing gown— a dangerous colour for messy people like me, but not a problem for anal personalities like her. Her hair was neatly contained in a bun. I didn't think I'd ever seen her dishevelled. "Yes, Ma'am. It was super loud, and I'd had enough."

She looked over my shoulder. "Settled in, I see. This reminds me of your Sydney apartment." She shook her head.

"Yeah, I know. I'm going to tidy up. Can you teach me how to do it magically? Pretty please?"

"Do you promise to keep your room tidy from now on if I teach you the spell?"

"Yes. I promise." There's no way I could've made that promise pre-magic, but if it took a few words and the wave of a hand, it should be easy-peasy to maintain. Who said a leopard couldn't change its spots?

"It's not hard, actually. All you have to do is envisage your things where you want them, then listen for the hum of power and say, 'So many things in a jumbled mess, make it clean enough to impress.'"

That sounded like the spell she'd used at my place in Cronulla. *Okay, here goes nothing.* I imagined all the clothes on my bed hung up, and the shoes neatly arranged at the bottom of my wardrobe. I shut my eyes and found the hum that underlined everything if you only took notice. Then I said, "So many things in a jumbled mess, make it clean enough to impress." My skin tingled. I opened my eyes. Holy crap! My bed was clear. I ran to the wardrobe and opened one door. My stuff was all there, just as I'd imagined! Wow. I jumped up and down. "Woohoo! I did it. Yay, me!"

Angelica laughed. "I told you it wasn't hard."

"Is most magic that easy?"

"Pretty much. Some things are hard, like travelling, and some spells can be pushed back to the caster, so you have to be careful what you do to other people, but honestly, Lily, you should be trying more things by now. I gave you the

Beginner's Book of Spells last week. Haven't you been reading it?"

"Well, yes, but I didn't think to try anything. I thought I had to wait for you to show me."

"There's nothing dangerous in that book, so get practicing. I want to see you do three more spells by Monday."

"Okay. And thanks." Three spells by Monday were totally doable. My boring weekend just got more interesting.

Now, what to pick? I happily thought about it as I drifted to sleep.

❦

By lunchtime Saturday, I'd learnt a cleaning spell. I know it didn't sound exciting, and trust me, if someone had told me one of the first spells I'd choose to learn was for housework, I would have laughed. We've established I didn't do it that much anyway. But, it was pretty awesome for two reasons. One was the obvious: goodbye scrubbing toilets and mopping floors. The other was that when you did the spell, you had to choose where the dirt would go. The toilet was easy: I imagined it in the sewerage pipes far away from the house, but dirt on the floors? I tested imagining it as a little pile outside the back door, and guess what? The little pile was there when I checked.

This opened up all sorts of interesting scenarios for having fun or getting payback. Someone being a pain in the arse? No problem. Just smear toilet grime on their behind. They wouldn't even notice until someone told them.

Someone bitching about you burning their coffee or giving them sticky change? Magic some dirt into their drink. They'd never know until it was too late. I had an inkling that magic wasn't meant to be used for that, but I wasn't about to let that stop me. I did promise myself I would only use it in emergencies. There had to be some boundaries, or I'd be out of control in no time.

In my excitement at magicking, I cleaned the whole house. Funnily enough, by the time I'd finished, I was tired. Not as tired as if I'd physically done everything, and it had only taken twenty minutes, but still tired enough that when I'd finished, I only just managed to make a coffee with the machine William gave me and slump into one of the armchairs in the living room.

Angelica was out, so I called her. "Hi, Ma'am."

"Hello, dear. How are you?"

"I'm good. I just cleaned the whole house... with magic!"

"Congratulations. Is that all you wanted to tell me? I'm just in the middle of something."

"Oh, sorry. No. I wanted to ask is it normal to be tired after doing lots of magic?"

"Yes, until you get used to it. It's like running: you start off weaker, and you get stronger as you go, but you're using your own energy to control the source magic, kind of like if you were standing in a stream and redirecting fast-flowing water. I have to go now. I'll see you tonight for dinner."

"Okay. Bye." The phone dropped out. Maybe I should read or something. I was tired but bored—that horrible in-between feeling where an unnameable irritation gnawed at your stomach. Normally if I felt like this, I'd call my friends, and we'd go into the city or for a coffee, but I didn't have any good friends here. Maybe I should call Millicent? I hadn't seen her for a while—she worked five days a week, and on the weekends, she and James did couple stuff.

I dialled Millicent anyway, but James answered. "Lily. How'd you go last night?"

I rolled my eyes. As if he hadn't heard I'd gotten home early and how I'd gotten home. "Fine, thanks. Is Mill there?"

"No, well, yes, but we're at the doctor. She's been a bit sick the last few of days. A stomach bug, I think. We're here to see if we can get her something for it." I heard retching in the background, and my stomach turned. I gagged. I was a sympathy vomiter. If I heard someone vomit or smelled vomit, I was done.

I spoke quickly. "Yeah. Tell her I hope she gets better soon. Bye." I hung up. If he wanted to tell me anything else, he could call me at a less gross moment. I so wasn't having kids. Nope. Poo and vomit were no-go zones. That cut out any idea of me having dogs too, and probably cats. Now I was sad. I liked animals. Ooh, maybe I could magic their poo into the sewer! Hmm, that could work.

Now what? Should I look into getting a car? There were so many things to see in England: castles, gardens, muse-ums, even beaches, although they weren't the beaches with soft golden sand I was used to, still, the sea was the sea. My bank account could stand me getting an older second-hand car. I could probably snag a semi-reliable car for two or three thousand pounds. But that was a bit too complicated for one afternoon. I'd figure it out later. Right now, I was bored, and I needed to do something.

Maybe taking photos would cheer me up. If I stuck to outside and avoided putting people in my sights, I'd avoid the dead-person thing. Shit. What if I saw someone at the engagement was going to die? What if it were Olivia or her parents? *Way to go, witches. You've taken something I loved and turned it into potential torture.* I'd have to never take photos of my brother or Millicent again. I didn't want prior knowledge. And what about selfies? My jaw dropped. I wasn't a serial selfie taker, but still. *Stop thinking, Lily. It's not helping. Breathe.* Maybe there was a way I could switch it off? Okay, I'd go with that thought and check with Angelica later.

I grabbed my camera and headed outside. Our laneway was just as quaint as the rest of Westerham, so I didn't have to wander far to get some nice pictures. I crossed the road and walked about fifty metres before turning and pointing the camera towards Angelica's property. The jasmine was flowering, and blue agapanthus grew in a row between the front fence and the road. *Click.*

I blinked. Goosebumps stole along my arms. Through the lens, the day had darkened to twilight, and a black van had popped into the scene, a couple of houses down from Angelica's. *Click.* It looked like the one that had pulled up behind me the day I was almost kidnapped. I swallowed and reminded myself they weren't here now. I walked towards it, my muscles tensed, camera still up—I didn't want to lose the image, but I was ready to run if I had to.

I stood in front of the van and pointed my camera at the two men in the front, who didn't have balaclavas on this time. The hair on the back of my neck stood on end. It was freaky. It was like they were really there, and I waited for them to notice me. Both men were bulky bastards, thick-necked and broad-shouldered. The driver's dark hair was short, and a snake tattoo slithered up his neck to hide under his black beard, the snake's tongue flicking out to almost touch his earlobe. He was laughing, which exposed crooked front teeth. The other guy was totally bald. His thick black eyebrows made little awnings above his dark eyes, or was that one awning? He had an aggressive monobrow going on. I scrunched my face. Not a good look.

Were these the guys who tried to snatch me, or were they just delivery guys taking a break? I was pretty sure I knew the answer to that question. My magic didn't do too many random things. There was a reason I was seeing this. When had they been here? And had they been here more than once, watching, waiting?

I looked around, suddenly cold, even though the sun was shining. It was about eighteen degrees today, so it wasn't warm, but it felt like the temperature had dropped to ten degrees. I walked around the van and took photos from every angle. I even reached out and tried to open the driver's door, but my hand met nothing. Well, it was worth a try.

Now was the time to test my phone theory. I turned my

camera off and switched my phone to camera mode. I listened for the hum of magic. "Show me the black van." Yep, there it was! So that answered that. I took the shot, just to make sure.

I dialled Angelica. "Hi, Ma'am."

"Calling again so soon?"

"Yes. I have something you need to see. I just took some photos outside your house, and the black van was there."

Her voice was frantic. "Goodness, Lily, get inside, now!"

"No, no, sorry. They're not here now. But they've been here before. I was able to get photos of their faces too." I shivered, wondering how often they sat out here, just waiting. Would they ever try and come inside when I was home alone? Angelica worked late some nights. Vulnerability didn't sit well with me. I needed to find spells to defend myself.

Heavy breathing came over the phone. "Goodness me. Don't scare me like that again. Get inside anyway. I'll be there in a jiffy."

I'd only just made it inside when Angelica came out of the reception room. We sat on a Chesterfield, and I handed her my camera. She scrolled through the photos. "These are very good, Lily." She shook her head. "What you do is amazing. And you have the number plate too. I'll get Tim to run these images through the system. We'll have a positive ID on these guys before you know it."

"But if we catch these guys and they aren't stalking me anymore, won't whoever's behind this just send someone else to watch me? At least these guys don't seem super competent, and we'll know who they are. Maybe we can do a reverse spy?"

She looked at me, her eyes wide, poker face gone. But then she regained her composure, and the serious expression was back. "That is an excellent idea. You sure you don't want a permanent job with us?"

"No thanks. Maybe if you were running things, I'd consider it, but not right now." I didn't trust the PIB. I could trust some of the people working there, but the guy running things, at least who was seen to be running things—because, let's face it, us little people rarely knew who was making the big decisions—Pembleton, didn't inspire confidence. He'd given his witch of a niece a job there, and she'd kidnapped my brother and almost killed me. Not too clever if you asked me.

"Well, I'll get the information on them so we know how to handle things. They're probably low-level witches, or their boss wouldn't have them doing something as mundane as following you."

"They did try and snatch me once."

"Without succeeding."

"True. If they wanted me dead, why wouldn't they just kill me from a distance?"

She stared at me, maybe assessing how to say what she wanted without freaking me out. "They may not want you dead. Your parents may not even be dead, Lily. They might want you to use your magic for them, or they might want you dead, but they're not ready to act yet. People like these have plans, Lily. And if anything happens to you, we'll be after them. I'm sure they don't want that kind of pressure, especially if they're working towards something. We need to find out who they are before whatever it is they're waiting for happens. Right now, we can't tie them to your parents' disappearance, so they can sit back and wait."

I tamped down the buzz of hope vibrating in my chest. Assuming they'd died was almost easier than hoping they were alive but knowing we'd been separated for so long when we could have been together. What if they were out there, somewhere, tortured, hoping, waiting to be saved? What if I could see them again? I took a deep breath. No, hoping like that only to have it annihilated later would kill me. I'd grieved their deaths, and there was no way I could do it again. Best to focus on what was real, here and now. "Could whoever they are be waiting to see if I'm a threat?"

"You mean waiting to see if you have your mother's talents?"

I nodded.

She shrugged. "Maybe." She took a memory card out of her pocket and handed it to me. "Your other one."

"Thanks."

Then she took the memory card out of my camera and pocketed that. "I'll get this back to you tonight. Will you be okay if I head back to the office now?"

"Yeah. I guess so." I tried not to sound sorry for myself. Living in England was not what I'd thought it would be. I wanted to visit castles and galleries, spend time with James and Millicent. Instead, I was dredging up the past and avoiding being kidnapped. I sighed. "See you tonight."

"Bye, Lily."

Alone. Again.

That was it. I wasn't going to sit around feeling sorry for myself. I grabbed my wallet. It was time to go into town, to the supermarket. *Double-choc-chip ice cream, here I come.*

CHAPTER 5

Olivia pulled out her phone. "Selfie time!" We stood on London Bridge. Menacing black clouds closed in around the Thames, but it wasn't raining. Yet. Red double-decker buses and black London cabs zoomed past. We were looking across the brownish-grey river at Tower Bridge. As pretty as the scene was, the river looked kind of dirty. Swimming was definitely out of the question, not to mention it was cold. Olivia turned around, putting her back to Tower Bridge. "Come on, Lily."

I turned around, and we leaned our heads together, smiling. She used her phone to take the shot, then checked it. "What do you think?" She showed it to me.

"Looks fine. No double chins. We're good. Can you message it to me?" There was no way I was getting my phone out and taking photos of us. It wasn't just the fear of taking a photo I didn't want to see, but what if something weird showed up, and Olivia saw the picture. How would I explain that extra person behind us that wasn't actually there, or the fact that someone was faint enough to see through?

I did have my Nikon with me—*let's not get crazy; it came with me almost everywhere*—and I snapped a few shots, because no one ever asked to see those. Nothing weird showed up. My shoulders relaxed, releasing the tension I didn't realise I harboured. The quicker I figured out how to turn my talent off, the better. I'd managed to learn another two spells on Sunday, as per Angelica's challenge. I could now magic an item to me or away from me, but I had to know what the item looked like, where it was, and I had to be able to imagine the place I was moving it to. The other super exciting thing I could do was dewrinkle my clothes without ironing. You'd be right if you thought that was beyond boring. There were even more mundane spells than that— I'd picked the more exciting ones from the beginner's book.

"What's that building over there? It looks like one of those old mobile phones, the really big ones."

"That's the Walkie Talkie."

"Ha! Cool name."

"It's not the official name, but that's what everyone calls it."

We walked to the other side and along the northern side of the Thames, towards Tower Bridge. There was a bit of a line to get tickets, but that was to be expected. Beyond the gatehouse, the bridge towers rose five stories and had character galore, having been built in the late eighteen-hundreds. Four turrets surrounded a main one on each of the two towers. I'd taken a handful of shots when the lighting changed. It switched to sunny, and walking towards me across the bridge was a procession of horses and carts, all driven by men with some kind of hat on—some wore berets, and some wore traditional wide-brimmed hats. Oh my God! This was amazing. There were no cars, just people dressed in olden-day clothes, and my picture was in colour. I swallowed. This was a big deal. Imagine the history I could uncover with my abilities. But no one would believe it wasn't Photoshopped. Bummer.

"Getting some good shots?"

I flicked the Off switch and let my camera dangle from the neck strap. "Ah, yeah. Great. Thanks for bringing me here. I imagine you've been here heaps of times."

She laughed. "I've had two school excursions and shown about four other people around, so you could say that. But I don't mind. I love history. I have a bachelor of arts in social anthropology and history."

"Can I be rude and ask why you're working at Costa?" Too bad if she didn't like the question; it was out there now. I wasn't exactly known for my tact. I hoped she wasn't offended.

She smiled. "It's not a rude question." *Phew.* "I can't decide where I want to take it next. I'm deciding between teaching and working at a museum. I'll be going back to study again next year, depending on what I decide, although I think it's easier to get a teaching job rather than a museum one. Plus, now that I'm marrying Ernie, I don't want to commit to too much. I really want to have kids soon, and his job's going really well, so we'll have that option."

Yeah, his theft was going great guns. Gah. I plastered the smile on my face. If we outed Ernest, all her dreams were going to go down the toilet. How could I do that to her? She was so nice. I guess I shouldn't get too close to her, because she was going to hate me when this was all over. She was so much better off without that jerk, but you couldn't tell someone that, especially someone you hardly knew. She had to find out for herself. My heart hurt for her. Stupid magic. Stupid Ernest, and stupid bloody Camilla.

We got our tickets and went to the upper level of the bridge that sat above where the road underneath opened. There were even glass panels in the floor. Wow. Looking down on the people and cars was cool, if a bit off-putting. You'd think I'd be an expert at dealing with weird crap by now, but I was a slow learner.

I'd read an entry in Mum's diary talking about her and Dad visiting Trafalgar Square and the art gallery there, so I'd asked Olivia if we could visit. I just told her my parents had been there before, because the diaries were still a secret. The only ones who knew they existed were me, Angelica, and James.

After Tower Bridge, we took the underground. The tube was packed but orderly. We made the trip without any problems. After a short walk from the tube station, we arrived at Trafalgar Square. The large paved area was surrounded by roads on three sides with the National Gallery overlooking Nelson's column—it was quite tall—

plus a statue with a horse, and a fountain. A couple of street artists drew chalk pictures on the pavement near the gallery. Tourists took photos, and workers in office gear hurried past.

Drops of water landed on my face, and I looked up. "It's raining."

"Let's get inside."

We hurried up the stairs and into the National Gallery, which was free. "Are you kidding? Nothing's free."

"Most of our galleries and museums are free."

"Ours aren't." Australia needed to get onboard with generosity. What a great idea, making tourists feel like they weren't getting ripped off. Novel idea. Plus, if you felt really guilty for getting something free, like I was sure to, you could buy a souvenir at the end, because what exhibit didn't end at a gift shop?

We wandered through high-ceilinged rooms, one of which had an impressive domed roof and gild-accented arches. Hushed voices echoed in the vast spaces. You could smell the history, that almost-musty yet sweet odour of old books and antique furniture.

We entered a new room, and I stopped in front of the first painting. Holy crap. It was one of my favourite artists— Canaletto. His renditions of Venice blew my mind. That's what I'd do in the next life: be an artist. Hmm, maybe I could take up painting again on the days I had nothing to do and didn't feel like confronting my camera. I'd enjoyed art at school but hadn't done any since. Something to think about.

Olivia stood next to me, our shoulders almost touching. "You ever been to Venice?"

"Yeah, once. My dad's family used to live near there. It was awesome, although it was so long ago, I've forgotten a lot of it. Photos help me remember." And that was for all things—not just holidays. If it weren't for photos, I'd lose my parents for good. "What about you?"

"Twice. My parents love to travel. We go somewhere different every year. It's easy when everything's so close."

"You're lucky. To get here from Australia takes at least twenty-four hours."

She looked at me and smiled. "But you're lucky now too. You live here. Hey, we should go on a long weekend somewhere together. Ernie often has to go to conferences for the weekend. We could go to Paris, Berlin, Rome. Wherever you want."

"That would be freaking awesome! I'd love to." I was close to everything now, so why not take advantage? I snorted: I wondered how Beren and William would like following me around Europe. Ha! Something else niggled at me, though. Oh, that's right, Ernie and his conferences. Conferences my arse. He was probably liaising with super-witch Camilla. I bet she was giving him presentations all right. Cow.

Gah, push out the negative thoughts and enjoy the moment. There was nothing I could do about it right now, so I stepped back from the Canaletto and framed a wide shot. As I clicked, two people, their backs to me, popped into the picture. They were holding hands. The woman was about my height, with shoulder-length wavy brown hair. The man stood a few inches taller. They wore jeans and shirts, casual gear. Something about them was familiar.

My mouth went dry, and my stomach dropped. It couldn't be. I kept the camera up and walked around them, so my camera was pointing at their faces, towards Olivia who stood behind them.

I froze for a moment, not even breathing, tears blurring my sight. I shook my head. It couldn't be. It just couldn't. My hands trembled as I clicked and clicked and clicked and clicked. I reached out one hand. *Please, please, please.*

But there was no one there.

I knew there wouldn't be, but I couldn't help it. My heart constricted, and I couldn't breathe.

"Lily, are you all right?"

I reluctantly lowered my camera, aware of the tears running down my face but not caring. I didn't want to stop looking through my camera, but I was sure my behaviour already seemed strange to my friend. "I don't feel well. Can we grab a water or something and sit?"

I thrashed against the panic threatening to drown me. It couldn't be, but it was.

I'd just seen my parents.

Nausea crawled up my throat. I made it to the garbage bin just in time.

Olivia rubbed my back. "Oh, no, you poor thing. Let's get you cleaned up, and we'll head home."

I nodded, grateful I wasn't alone. All the walls I'd built, all the progress I'd made since my parents had disappeared was destroyed in an instant. I was that fourteen-year-old girl again, crying myself to sleep every night, comforting my brother who cried almost as much as I did for weeks, until he got it together. It had taken me longer, but I'd done it. Now all that healing had been undone, sliced to pieces by my own damn magic.

A wound so bloody and painful had opened, spilling my insides onto the shiny gallery tiles. Olivia led me out, and I wondered how they were going to clean my blood off the floor.

There was no way I was ever using magic again.

Ever.

CHAPTER 6

We caught the train back, and Olivia drove me home from the station. I'd tried to perk up, but it was no use. Seeing my parents was too much of a shock. Guilt jumped onto the fresh grief that was just as bad as it had been way back when. Olivia had shown me such a lovely time, and then I stuffed everything up.

I'd ruined our day in London.

We arrived at Angelica's. I pushed the car door open and got out. "I'm so, so sorry, Olivia. Thanks for taking me. I really appreciate it."

"Hey, Lily, it's okay. I'm just sorry you're so sick. Call me tomorrow. Let me know if you're feeling better." Sympathy shone from her eyes.

"I will. Drive safe." I shut the car door and made my way to the house. When I walked in, Angelica, James, and Millicent were waiting in the living room.

Millicent ran to me. "Are you okay, Lily? Oh goodness. You're so pale. Sit down." She grabbed my arm and steered me to one of the Chesterfields.

I couldn't even manage a half smile. "What are you guys doing here?"

James stared at me. "Waiting for you. Millicent picked up on your feelings. She said it was serious, so we came here."

How had she sensed my thoughts? "But I shielded myself this morning."

Millicent answered. "Your emotions send off a different signal to your thoughts. The mind-protection spell doesn't cover feelings."

"Oh." Well, what difference did it make, since I wasn't going to do magic anymore? "I suggest you all sit down, and then look at my photos." James frowned, probably at the look on my face. "Olivia took me to the National Gallery today. I'm sorry."

What else could I say? I was about to put my brother and Angelica through a world of hell. But they would want me to show them. I was sure of it.

I sat and put my head in my hands and cried. I'd held it in as much as I could on the train, but I couldn't hold back now. My parents. My beautiful, loving, giving parents. The ones I'd never hug, never talk to, never celebrate birthdays or Christmas with. Ever again. They'd been right there. I could have touched them. But I couldn't. They were phantasms. As ephemeral as a dream.

Millicent gasped, and Angelica said, "Oh, my God." I

looked up. James sat in the middle, and they all stared at the screen. James looked as sick as I felt, his skin white, eyes glassy. Tears ran down his cheeks. Millicent threw her arms around him and squeezed. Angelica looked up at me, her eyes glistening with unshed tears. Then she did something I'd never have expected. She stood, came over, and wrapped her arms around me.

"Oh, Lily. I'm so sorry." We sobbed together.

After we'd cried enough to exhaust ourselves, I stood. I enclosed James's hands in mine. "Time to turn that off. I'll put it on my laptop tomorrow, and we can see it more clearly, but for now, I think we should talk." He let me pry the camera from his hands, and I turned it off. His forlorn eyes met mine, and I struggled not to start weeping all over again.

He shook his head, his shoulders dropping. "How could you handle seeing them? Right there? Are you going to be okay?"

"I lost it and threw up in a bin, and I didn't care. Olivia must have thought I was a nut. To be honest, I can't remember much except staring at them, wanting to touch them so bad. I'm surprised at how many photos I took. I was on automatic pilot." I took a shuddering breath. "I feel like I've lost them all over again."

James nodded. "Me too."

I sat next to him and held his hand. "I don't want to be a witch anymore. I don't think I can handle seeing them again."

Angelica's voice was soft. "I'm sorry, Lily, but you don't

have that option. You can't stop being a witch. You can stop using your magic, but it will always call to you. And the more you don't use it, the greater the need will be."

Noooooo! It felt like my heart was being squeezed into oblivion. "Can I at least turn it off, so I can't see things when I take photos?" My one passion was turning into a freaking nightmare.

She thought for a moment. "I do believe that's possible. James, you can turn off your lie detecting, can't you?"

"If I try hard enough, yes. Sometimes I need a break from knowing everything, or I just want to relax with friends, and I don't want to be judging every conversation."

She turned to Millicent. "What about you, dear?"

"Yes. I can stop picking up on what everyone else is feeling, but I don't like to, because I feel isolated. But it's possible. I also have to cut myself off from all magic. It's a bit scary, to be honest. I worry I'll lose it forever when I do that. It's like stepping into a lifeless void. Lily, don't make any rash decisions while you're upset, although you can't run from your powers anyway. Just hang in there. We'll be here for you, I promise." She gave me an encouraging smile, then took a deep breath. "I'm not sure if this is the right time to tell you, but we have some news."

A ghost of a smile touched James's lips before sadness swept it away. "You can tell them, Mill."

Happiness shone from her eyes. "You know how I was sick the other day?" I nodded. "It turns out that I'm pregnant. We're having a baby." Her smile of pure joy cheered me up. My parents would have loved this, but they would never get to hold their grandbabies. Bittersweet sucked. Couldn't we just do away with the bitter?

My no-hugs policy went out the window as I bear hugged both Millicent and James. "You guys, that's awesome. I'm so happy for you." And then I was crying again, but this time, they were happy tears.

"My, what a day!" Angelica clapped her hands once. "I think this calls for a cup of tea."

"And a coffee?"

"Of course, Lily. I'll magic you up a cappuccino from your favourite investigator's coffee machine."

I laughed. "Very funny, Ma'am."

Two teacups on saucers and filled with water and a teabag appeared on the table that sat between the Chesterfields. Angelica waved her hand over them until steam rose. The screaming hiss of milk frothing came from the kitchen. Two cappuccinos appeared on the table. Both had chocolate on the top in the shape of a heart. Aw, that was so sweet. "Thank you, Ma'am. I think you're my favourite witch ever."

"Hey, what about me?" asked James.

"And me!" Millicent pouted.

"Stuff it. You're all my favourites." Because, really, how could I choose? They'd all been there for me, and would always be. No matter how many meltdowns I had, they'd be here to help me pick up the pieces. "Thanks, guys. I don't know what I'd do without you."

"I'll drink to that." Millicent raised her teacup, her pinkie finger elegantly sticking out.

"Here's to babies and family." I raised my coffee, and we all clinked our cups together.

I hated having to stay the witch course, but if what they all said was true, I didn't have a choice. "Ma'am, since it seems like I'm stuck with being a witch, can you start teaching me tomorrow how to cut off the power?"

She turned a resigned gaze on me. "If you insist. We can start tomorrow."

"Thank you." Relief stormed through my body, leaving exhaustion in its wake. Even the smell and taste of coffee wasn't enough to hold it at bay. I mustered up enough energy to finish the coffee—this was me we were talking about—and I hugged everyone again.

"Can I borrow the memory card?" James asked.

"Of course."

"I don't want you to send me the photos, because anyone could intercept them, and then your secret will be out."

"But how will anyone know when they were taken?"

"True, but best to be safe rather than sorry."

Angelica magicked everyone's empty cups away. "I'll need a copy too, for the file. But I can do that here. It's too risky to take into the PIB."

That surprised me. I thought I was the only one who didn't trust that organisation. Looked like I was in good company.

"I'll back this up on a memory stick and give this back to you tomorrow. Okay?"

"Yep, that's fine. But please be careful with it. I don't

want to go through getting those photos again. As much as it hurts to see them, it would hurt to lose that extra little piece we've got."

He gave me a sad smile. "I know. I'll be careful."

"Well, today's beaten me, so I'm off to bed. And congrats again." I left them with a smile. From now on, I would try and focus on what I had rather than what I didn't. Hopefully it wouldn't be as hard as I feared.

CHAPTER 7

I t was Friday night. I sat in my favourite chair next to the fireplace, even though there was no fire, in my fleecy tracksuit and Ugg boots. My iPod was turned up while I read a cosy mystery on my iPad. I loved those books, and this author was particularly funny.

Was that a voice? I could never hear much with the earphones in. I took one out.

"Lily, dear, are you home?"

"Yes, Ma'am. In here!" It was about time for her to come home from work. She usually worked until at least 7:00 p.m., sometimes later.

I looked around the back of my chair. She came in, William and Beren on her heels. I took the other earphone out, turned my iPod off, and stood. "Are we having a party or something?" I frowned. "Where's the cake?"

Beren grinned, and William shook his head. Yes, I was

kidding, but my lack of social life was no joke. I totally needed to sign up to a local art class to meet more people.

Angelica sat on one of the Chesterfields. "Come over here, dear. We need to have a chat." Why do people say that? Everyone knows that's interchangeable with *I know you won't want to have this conversation, and you're going to hate what I have to say, but we're going to anyway. This is supposed to soften the blow, but it actually won't.*

William sat next to her, and Beren sat on the opposite lounge. I sat next to him.

Angelica smiled, as if she were trying to butter me up for something. She held out her hand, and a frothy cappuccino appeared. She handed it to me. *Here we go.* I could smell manipulation a mile away, especially when it was sprinkled with chocolate and full of caffeine.

"Lily, you've got your first photography job tomorrow. Is that right?"

Okay, this had something to do with Ernest, but what? I took the coffee—I wasn't *that* disgusted. "Yes. But if you want me to do something, please don't beat around the bush. Just ask." I hated bullshit. I didn't dish it out, and I sure as hell didn't like being on the other end of it. Honesty could hurt, but I was a rip-the-Band-Aid-off kind of person. Face the pain, and get it over with.

Her smile was genuine this time. "That's my Lily. Sorry. I'm used to dealing with… different people. We still need to find out if Camilla spelled her employee to help her, and we're short of evidence linking her directly with the crimes. We've tried a couple of different ways, but with no success.

The only thing that'll work is us getting close enough to put hands on him and find out if he's been spelled. Then we can figure out a new approach from there. Our research has indicated he's engaged to your new friend from the coffee shop, the one you're photographing for this weekend. Am I right?"

My eyes widened. Of course they'd find out. So much for giving myself some space to decide how I was going to keep my connection with Olivia out of it. I sighed. "Yes, you're right."

She pressed her lips together. "How long have you known, dear?"

"Since I went out with them the other Friday night. I'm sorry I didn't tell you. I was just figuring out how it would work. Me being friends with Olivia complicates things. Maybe I should step aside from this investigation?"

She shook her head. "I'm afraid not, Lily. We need your help, and those poor people they've stolen from deserve a resolution and justice. You're our best chance at getting close to him without having to resort to being obvious."

How was it, even when I was treading carefully, I still ended up knee deep in a cowpat? "You want me to put my hands on him? I can't do that. How would I explain that to Olivia if someone walked in? Not to mention, I have no idea how to find out if a spell's been cast on someone."

Angelica put her hand up. "Not you, Lily. Don't worry. I wouldn't ask you to do something I hadn't taught you. I'd like you to take an assistant to your photo shoot."

She closed her mouth, like she was holding her breath. I

narrowed my eyes, then looked at Beren. He smiled. I looked at William, who attempted a smile. It was kind of lame, but the fact that he'd tried meant something was going on. *Oh no.* "No, no, no, no, no. I'm not taking William as my assistant. Nope." I shook my head.

Angelica dug deep and found her poker face. "Now, Lily, don't say no without thinking about it. You want to help all those people who were swindled, don't you? Also, what if we arrest him when it wasn't even his fault. How would you feel? I'm sure your friend wouldn't be happy if he wrong-fully ended up in jail."

Ooh, that was a low blow, bringing my loyalty to Olivia into it. Not only did I hate going behind her back to poten-tially get her fiancé arrested, but there was also no way William and I could get along for a few hours. It was hard enough not to argue with him when we spent five minutes together. I took a deep breath. "You're putting me in a crappy position, but I hate knowing Camilla stole from people, and I suppose if he's guilty, he deserves to be charged, and if he's innocent, he deserves to be exonerat-ed." I glanced at William before looking back at Angelica. "Are you sure this is the only way?"

She nodded.

"Okay. I'll do it, under duress, mind you. But I have one condition: Beren can be my assistant, not William."

William folded his arms, his face smug. "Sorry, Lily. No can do. Beren can't wipe memories. It takes a minute or two to cast a detect spell and decipher the results, so, unless you can come up with a good reason for Beren having his hands on Ernest for one minute, feel free to tell me now. I'm just as keen as you to avoid being your assistant, so I'm open to suggestions."

"James can wipe memories. Can't he come instead?"

Angelica shook her head. "Unfortunately, no. He's investigating another case, and we can't take him off it. Surely you're adult enough to get along nicely for three or four hours?"

William and I looked at each other. I folded my arms, imitating him, then raised one brow. He raised one brow. Gah. "Okay. You all win. But if one of us doesn't make it out alive, I'm not taking any responsibility."

Angelica smiled, no doubt because she'd gotten her way. "Don't be so dramatic. All you have to do is your job and let William decide when and where he gets his information."

Easy for her to say. They thought they'd had the last laugh. I smirked. "Fine." They'd totally underestimated me.

Game on.

❦

ALL MY CAMERA EQUIPMENT WAS PACKED... IN THREE BAGS. I had four different lenses, two cameras, spare batteries, tripod, reflector, dropdown background, and lighting. I wouldn't normally take all that stuff, but if William wanted to be my helper, he was going to help until it hurt.

I magicked it all downstairs before I joined it, the normal way. William was waiting in the vestibule, looking way too sexy in denim jeans and a navy polo neck that gave entirely too much information on how built his chest was. The colour also brought out the blue in his eyes. I slapped myself across the cheek. *Bad, Lily. You don't like him, remember?* He looked at me like he was worried about my mental health—and he was probably right to be concerned. That was a crazy thing to do, but I was beyond caring. He looked me up and down. "I thought this was an engagement, not a funeral."

Smart arse. "I happen to like wearing black. Plus it singles me out as someone no one should talk to. When I'm working, I don't like to make small talk." Well, I rarely liked to any time, but more so when I was concentrating on getting the right shot.

His eyes widened slightly, and his mouth turned up on one side. Crap. I'd basically just told him how to annoy me. But then he eyed all the equipment on the floor, and his small smile vanished.

"What's wrong, *helper?*"

He ignored me and waved his hand. My stuff vanished. "Car's packed. Let's go." He turned, and I followed him out to the Range Rover.

I hopped into the front passenger seat. This was different. I was normally in the back exchanging angry glances in the mirror. Now I could shut him out by looking out the window. I turned to check the back, and my equipment was there, peeking over the top of the back seats.

I'd written the address on a piece of paper, which I handed to William. "Okay, Lily. Should take about ten minutes."

As he drove, I got the lecture. "Rule number one: don't do anything witchy in front of anyone. Rule two: let me do what I need to and don't get upset. Rule three: don't interfere. Rule four: if I ask you to do something, don't argue. Just do it."

"Um, shouldn't rule four be the other way around? You're my assistant. If you don't act the part, people are going to wonder why the hell you're there. And I don't want anyone thinking I pay you to do nothing."

"Why would that be?"

I rolled my eyes. He knew why. "*Some* people, not me mind, but some people, probably think you're good-looking. I don't want *those* people thinking I'd employ someone just so I could hang out with them and perv. I'm not a sucker." I gave him my I-hate-you face, just so we were clear.

He sniggered. "Yeah, *some* people. I'm pretty sure, you're *some* people."

"Don't flatter yourself. I may've thought you were attractive when I first met you, but since then, I've gotten to know you." Score one for me.

"Ouch." He grimaced, but thankfully, he kept any response to himself. We drove the rest of the way in blessed silence.

We arrived at the address, which was down another cute lane—England was full of them—to a formal iron gate with a lion crest on both brick pillars. The part of the driveway visible through the gates ran under a tunnel of foliage created by trees on both sides of the roadway. Swanky. I wondered if I'd written the address down correctly.

William rolled his window down and pressed the intercom. It buzzed, and a voice came through. "Can I help you?"

"Lily Bianchi photographer to see Olivia Grosvenor."

The gates started opening. "How did you know her last name? I didn't tell you. Hell, I didn't even know it. Although she filled in my online form, I didn't pay attention."

"Really, Lily? It's my job to know these things. And by the way, you should pay more attention. One day, you'll get yourself into trouble for not being thorough enough."

"Yes, Dad."

He gave me cranky side eyes. Well, if he didn't like being called "dad," he needed to be less bossy.

Five hundred metres down the driveway, the house finally appeared. A sprawling two-storey Edwardian-style brick home, majestic and surrounded by formal gardens, greeted us. A few rows of cars were parked on the grass. Wow, this was going to be a huge gathering. How had she not booked a proper photographer before me? It didn't look like money was an option. She must really love her cousin.

William followed the sweeping driveway and stopped in front of the front doors. Catering trucks were lined up around the circular return, which surrounded a fountain of a cherub pouring water out of a pitcher.

"Wow."

William looked at me. "You didn't know your friend was rich?"

"No. I've never been here before, and she works at Costa. Not exactly what you imagine an heiress would do.

Besides, her family is rich, not her. She wouldn't own this house." Maybe she had an older brother who would inherit all this. That sounded archaic, but who knew how things worked over here? I sure didn't.

I grabbed one of the three bags and watched as William struggled with the other two plus the reflector, tripod, and backdrop—it took him three tries to load up without dropping anything. Cruel of me, I knew, but he needed to know not to mess with me next time. There were consequences.

The front door was open, and just as I reached the threshold to call out, Olivia appeared and gave me a huge hug. "I'm so glad you made it! I can't wait for you to meet my family. And you look so much better."

"Yeah, it was some twenty-four-hour thing, but I'm much better now. Thanks. I've never seen your hair down." Her curls fell over her shoulders, stopping just under them. "Red lipstick is totally your colour."

I admired women who could wear red lipstick. If I tried, I looked like a clown.

"Thanks, Lily!" She looked over my shoulder. "I didn't know you had an assistant." She lowered her voice. "And quite a hot one at that."

"Oh, that's just William. He's studying photography." I turned as he almost tripped up the stairs trying not to drop the rolled-up backdrop. "Be careful. That stuff's expensive."

The look he gave me wouldn't be out of place on an enraged bear. Funny how that made me want to laugh.

I followed Olivia through high-ceilinged rooms filled with antique and designer furniture—the kind you see in those country-living-type magazines, to the back garden. I felt a little intimidated knowing no one as financially challenged as me probably ever stepped foot in this house unless they were fixing or catering something. One of the rooms we passed was bigger than my whole Sydney apartment. How was Olivia so down to earth?

Stone paving led from the house for about three metres before meeting the grass. Hedges framed the garden borders, and animal topiaries dotted the lawn: a squirrel, horse, dog, and elephant. A large marquee had been set up in the middle of the yard. There must have been at least two hundred people, both sitting under the tarp at tables and milling around outside in the sun. Children ran around, two Scottish terriers joining in. On the back patio, just to my left, was an honest to goodness champagne fountain. Black-clothed wait staff wandered around, offering trays of delicious-looking canapés to guests. Being the other half, or was that 1 per cent, was obviously awesome.

I looked back at William. "Maybe just stack the stuff there"—I pointed to the back wall—"and come with me. I'll have a look around and decide where I'm going to set up. Plus I'll have to introduce you to the *lucky* man." Lucky was a matter of opinion if we found out he was Camilla's willing accomplice. If I flipped a coin, would it tell me what the outcome would be? Why couldn't that be my magical talent? Last night, I'd gone over the cut-off-magic spell with Angelica so many times, if I got it wrong, it would be because I was epically stupid. I was cloaking my thoughts— just in case William could read them—but when I cut off my magic, my thoughts would be exposed. William reading my mind scared me only slightly less than seeing things I didn't want to see by accident. There was no getting around it: today was going to suck.

"And I want to introduce you to my parents." Olivia grinned.

"You look gorgeous, by the way," I said. Her white and floral-print dress was sleeveless with a scoop neck, fitted to the waist, then flared out fifties style. It was bright and happy, just like Olivia.

"Thanks! It took me ages to find it. I don't normally wear dresses. I must have tried on at least twenty before this one."

"Good luck finding a wedding dress." I laughed.

"Yeah, thanks. Maybe you can come with me when I look."

And didn't I feel like crap. What if I helped ruin her chance to marry Ernest? "I'd love to. Just tell me when and where, and I'm there. But what about your friends?" She must have other friends, ones she knew way better than me?

"One of my best friends just had a baby, like a week ago, and the other one is in Italy studying fashion design and textiles. They'll be fine to come to my wedding, but they couldn't make it today, and they won't be around to help me shop for my gown." She frowned.

Well, looked like I came along at the right time, or not. Not only would she not have her best friends here to help her through the shock of finding out her fiancé was a cheating criminal, she wouldn't even have her fiancé. I

DIONNE LISTER

suppressed a cringe as acidic guilt dissolved holes in my stomach lining. I was the last person she should be choosing to go dress shopping with.

She grabbed my hand and led me to the marquee, to a distinguished-looking couple standing together but talking to separate groups of people—I guessed there was never enough time at things like this to talk to everyone, so you had to do what you could, especially when you had hundreds of guests.

They were dressed in tailored clothes that were clearly designer. Her mother had her hair in a chic chignon that could have only been done by a hairdresser, but her smile was genuine, and there wasn't any sign of plastic surgery on her pretty forty-something-year-old face. She had the same warm brown eyes as her daughter.

"Mum, Dad, this is Lily, the photographer I was talking to you about, and this is her assistant, William. Lily, William, this is Robert and Cassandra." We all shook hands, and I smiled, hoping I was making a good impression.

"Lovely to meet you," said her mother. "I've heard so much about you. And don't you two make a gorgeous couple." She beamed.

I tried to mask the horror that was surely radiating from my face. "Oh, no. William's just my assistant. He's more like a big brother to me."

"Oh. I'm so sorry. Please forgive me." Cassandra blushed.

"Don't worry about it," said William. "I've always said we'd make a good couple, but Lily won't hear of it. She

88

broke my heart the first day I met her by turning me down, but I live in hope." He placed one hand over his heart and looked at me with a syrupy gaze, head tilted to the side. He was such a dirty fighter.

But I could be too. "I know where I'd love to set up for the first lot of formal pictures! By the topiaries at the end of the garden." The farthest point from the back of the house. Good luck with that, Will. "The light isn't too harsh there, and it's so pretty. Would you like to do them now? We can do some other ones later, and in between, I'll just flit around taking shots of the party. Olivia, would you mind rounding up Ernest, his parents, and any siblings you both have?"

"Not a problem, Lily."

"It was lovely to meet you both. Thank you for trusting me with your daughter's engagement photos."

Olivia's dad smiled. "She spoke so highly of you, and we checked out your website. Your work speaks for itself."

"Thank you." I smiled. What a nice thing to say. "William and I will go and grab what we need, and we'll see you at the topiaries in a minute."

As William and I returned to the back patio, I swallowed my fear and whispered the spell to cut off my magic. I hoped my thoughts stayed away from anything that could embarrass me in front of William.

I schooled my brain to blank and grabbed the bag with the camera I was going to use. It was time to focus on taking good pictures.

"Do you need all this?" William looked at the equipment on the ground.

"Yes. All of it, please." I lowered my voice. "And you're such an arse."

He grinned. "I try."

Argh! We'd only been here ten minutes, and I already wanted to throw champagne in his face.

"Just try, Lily." He had a wicked gleam in his eye. My mouth dropped open. He was spying on my thoughts already. It had taken him, what, all of five seconds? I narrowed my eyes. *You bastard! Keep out of my head.* He actually smirked. Was he trying to get himself defenestrated? Shame we weren't on the first floor. Who knew not seeing surprise future dead people in your photos was not worth the pain of cutting off your ability to protect your thoughts.

The topiaries were about seventy metres from the house —not far enough, if you asked me. After William laid everything on the ground, I set up my tripod, then took my camera out. I had the fifty-millimetre lens on—my favourite for portraits. I loved blurring out backgrounds.

"William, I'll need you to hold the reflector, thanks." I may as well make him useful, for real.

Olivia led her fiancé and the rest of their families over. Ernest had his arm around her. If I didn't know the truth, there's no way I would've picked up on the fact that he wasn't happy with her. If I found out he was cheating on purpose, he was going down, Lily style—he'd wish the police had gotten to him first.

Ernest held his hand out and greeted William. "Hey, man, thanks for coming to our engagement. I hear you're going to take some great pics." *What the?*

William squeezed his hand so hard, Ernest winced. "Lily's the photographer. I'm just her lowly helper." He smiled at me. Why did he have to go and be nice? Now I'd feel bad if I tortured him more. He winked. *I take it back.*

For the next twenty minutes, I got to work, directing people where to stand, when to smile, when to look serious, and William did an okay job with the reflector. Not that holding it up how I asked required a genius, but I wouldn't have been able to do it myself. If I got busier, I should look at getting a real assistant. I just couldn't afford one right now.

After we'd shot the first lot of portraits, instead of helping me pack up, William approached Ernest. "Hey, man. I need some advice. You seem to have some skill with the ladies, and I have a problem I was hoping you could help me with."

Ernest grinned and clapped Will on the back. "Hey, no problem." He turned to Olivia. "Babe, I'm just going to have a quick chat with my new friend." They turned towards the house. How long was it supposed to take? One minute, two? What if someone caught him and wondered what he was doing? I supposed he had an excuse, but then he'd have to wipe two people's memories. This could get complicated. I could at least help by making sure Olivia stayed out here.

"Hey, Olivia. Do you want to see some of the shots?"

"I'd love to! And call me Liv. All my friends do."

Aw, how sweet. She thought we were friends too. I would have enjoyed the moment more if I didn't know what might be coming. "I'll edit them of course, so they'll look even better. Let me know what you think."

I handed her the camera and let her scroll through. It was such a relief to not have to worry about weirdness popping into the photos. "Oh, my. These are amazing! I knew you'd come through." With unexpected speed, she executed a move designed to give me no chance at avoidance. She launched herself at me and squished me in a hug.

I stiffened and laughed awkwardly. "It's my job to be awesome."

She dropped her hands and stepped back before handing me my camera. Yay, I could breathe again.

"They're beyond my expectations, even unedited. My parents are going to love them." She looked towards the house, and her smile fell. I turned.

Ernest ran out of the back door, although it was more of a large opening, care of those accordion-type French doors. His hair was mussed up, and he looked like a kid who'd just hurt himself and needed a hug. What the hell had happened? I stared at the back door, waiting for William to appear. My mouth went dry.

Ernest kept his voice just above a whisper when he reached us, but the panicked overtone was clear. "I've had to call an ambulance. Something's happened to William." He looked at me and shook his head slowly.

I stopped breathing, and my stomach dropped. "Is he…?"

Ernest looked at me blankly. Oh, Christ, he was going to

make me say it out loud. "Is he"—I swallowed—"dead, badly hurt, bleeding out? What, damn you? Speak."

"I'm not even sure what happened. One minute he was asking whether he should ask you out on a date, and then there was some kind of a flash, and the next thing I know, I'm staring down at William lying on the ground."

I ran for the house, fumbling my phone out of my pocket as I went. Once inside, I had no idea where to go. If William wanted to have a private conversation, there's no way he would've had it in the main living area. I found a hallway and followed it, running into one room, then another.

Shit. I stopped and ripped down the barrier holding my magic at bay. Without even thinking, I envisaged standing in the river of power, drawing it up through my legs, into my body. I pictured William's intense grey-blue eyes. I whispered, "My friend is in trouble. Show me where he is, on the double."

An invisible force pulled me further down the hallway then to a door on the right that was wide open. There he was, lying on his back, unmoving. William! I sprinted to him and fell to my knees. I put my cheek against his mouth. He was breathing, thanks be to all the gods. I sat up. What was that weird smell? Burnt hair? His eyebrows were singed.

"William. William, can you hear me?" He didn't respond. I laid my hand on his cheek, rough with whiskers already growing through after this morning's shave. We had our differences, but I didn't want anything to happen to him, and if I were being totally honest, I had a small crush on him.

I dialled Angelica as sirens sounded in the distance. "Angelica?"

"What is it, Lily?"

"William's been hurt. I have no idea what happened, but I found him in the study lying on the ground, and his eyebrows are singed. He still has them, but they have those little melted balls on the end."

"Is he breathing?"

"Yes. I can't see anything else wrong, but he won't wake up. Ernest was with him when it happened. He's called an ambulance. They're almost here." The sirens were closer. "Angelica? It's your turn to talk. Hello?" *Don't leave me now.* Dread, metallic and sickly, clogged my throat and coated my tongue.

"Sorry, dear, just thinking. Go with him to the hospital. Call me when you know where you're going, and I'll be there with James in a jiffy. We have a cubicle in every hospital."

"Okay. Do you think this was caused by—"

"There you are. Oh my goodness, Lily. The ambulance is coming up the drive." Olivia rushed over and rubbed my back. I grabbed William's hand—it was still warm, thankfully—and looked up at Olivia. Ernest appeared behind her, looking genuinely sorry and confused.

"I'm so sorry, Liv, but I'm going to go to the hospital with him. I won't charge you for today." I hated letting her down, but William was more important. There was no way I could concentrate on work knowing he could be dying in hospital, alone.

"Don't worry. My cousin will be excited to have a turn at taking photos. I'll have your stuff packed into William's car. You can come get it later. Okay?"

"Thanks. You're one in a million."

"That's what friends are for."

I blinked traitorous wet stuff from my eyes and gave her a small smile.

The doorbell chimed. Ernest left but returned swiftly, followed by two paramedics. I stepped back and let them do their work. It was only in the ambulance, as I sat holding William's hand pleading for a miracle, that I realised I'd called Ma'am by her name. I'm sure she would understand there were extenuating circumstances. What a stupid thing to be worrying about. I shook my head and stared at William's unresponsive face. Gone were the wrinkles that were usually embedded in his forehead, and his strong jaw was relaxed. He looked kind of sweet when he wasn't angry. *Please wake up, Will.*

I bit my lip. Yep, calling Ma'am Angelica was nothing. We all had way more to worry about. What if Will died?

The ambulance slowed, but then the driver put the siren on. The ambulance jumped the median strip, jostling all of us around in the back. *Please make it in time.*

Please.

CHAPTER 8

As soon as we arrived at the hospital, they wheeled the still-unconscious William away. I found a chair in the crowded emergency waiting room and dialled Angelica. "Hi, Ma'am."

"How is he?" Concern weighed in her voice.

"Not good. He hasn't regained consciousness. We're at Princess Royal University Hospital. They've taken him for tests." I bit my fingernail. Gross habit, but something I was prone to when stressed.

"We'll be there in a minute. Are you in the waiting room?"

"Yes. See you soon." The line cut off.

A baby started crying, and I resisted the urge to cover my ears with my hands. My phone pinged with a message. It was from Olivia. I still felt so bad about abandoning her, but it wasn't even a choice.

Let me know when you have some news. Ernie says he's so sorry. If you need anything, let me know. Liv xx.

Thanks. Just waiting for them to run some tests, and it wasn't Ernest's fault. Sorry again about leaving. I hope you get to enjoy the rest of your party. Xx

But had it been? Or was it Camilla's fault, or something random? I was sure once Angelica arrived, we'd have more answers.

The baby was still crying when a minute later, Angelica, Beren, James, and a leggy brunette came from the direction of the toilets. I thought William didn't have a girlfriend? She looked like a freaking supermodel—at least five foot nine, slim with an elegant way of moving that had captivated at least half the poor sods in the waiting room… including me. Her dark locks were styled in loose waves that fell to her waist, and she made jeans and T-shirt look like a million bucks. Don't get me started on her stunning-even-without-make-up face. Well, if he had a girlfriend, at least she was worth losing to. Hang on. Where did that come from? He was the last person I should want to date. *Get a grip, Lily.* It must be the shock of seeing him struck down. Yep, I was going with that.

Angelica peeled away from the group and approached the reception. I stood and accepted a quick hug from Beren. "Hey. Are you okay?"

I nodded and resisted the urge to cry. There was no use being a mess until we knew what the prognosis was.

James introduced the stunner. "Lily, this is Will's sister,

Sarah." I should not feel as relieved as I did, especially when the poor girl looked as worried as I felt.

"Hi, Lily. It's nice to finally meet you. William mentioned you once."

Once? Okay. That wasn't exactly an endorsement. "Um, okay. It's nice to meet you too."

She lifted her hand to her mouth in such a floaty way: it was like she was in a music video, and she wasn't even trying. Sigh. "I'm so sorry. I didn't mean it like that. He never talks about anyone, let alone women, and he's not much of a talker to start with. That was actually a huge compliment." She smiled, revealing perfectly straight, super-white teeth.

I laughed. "Yep, that sounds like William." Come to think of it, he'd never mentioned he had a sister, but then again, he wasn't trying to be my friend. Acquaintances didn't bother sharing that information. I looked at my shoes and ignored the uncomfortable little squeeze of my heart.

Angelica joined us. "Come with me. They're letting us use a private lounge on the second floor while we wait." She looked around at the coughing, groaning, crying, and, in one case drunk, occupants of the room. Her lips pressed together, and her nose twitched. This must be her displeased expression while in poker-face mode.

We were buzzed into the section you only get into once you're admitted, and Angelica led us to a lift. I hurried to keep up with her. "How did you manage to swing a private room?"

She looked at me as if to say *Really? We're witches.*

Remember? Yes, I totally got all that from one raised-eyebrow glance.

We got into the lift. "So, what now?" Hopefully this question wasn't as stupid as the last one.

"James will sort everything out once we have some privacy." Angelica's authoritative tone soothed my nerves. At least someone who knew what they were doing was in charge.

The lift dinged, and we exited. Angelica turned right. We hit the end of the section of hallway where it doglegged right. A few doors down was one labelled Private Lounge. It wasn't plush, but it had comfortable-looking vinyl armchairs, a TV, sink, coffee-and-tea-making facilities, and a small basket full of toys in the corner next to a bright-red child-size table and two chairs.

"Now what?" Sarah asked. It just occurred to me that she must be a witch too. I wondered if she used a spell to stay slim. An anti-hungry spell would be awesome. I'd have to ask Angelica if it were possible.

James mumbled a few words. A white doctor's coat with ID hanging from the pocket appeared over his jumper and jeans, and a stethoscope dangled around his neck. *Impressive.*

"Nice threads. Totally believable."

"Thanks, sis."

I had to ask. "So what now?"

"I'm going to find William and do an examination. I'll only need a few minutes to figure out what happened. I'd bet anything, he got hit with a spell when he was delving into Ernest's thoughts. But I'll let you know everything when I get back. See you soon."

"Be careful," I called as he walked out.

Beren and Sarah had taken seats next to each other and held hands. She must be so worried. I know how I felt when James was missing. I never wanted to feel like that again. I went over to them. "Sarah, he'll be okay. James will do whatever it takes to figure this out."

"Thanks, Lily. I can't imagine not having him around. He's so strong, always there when I need him. We were close growing up, and my parents would die if anything happened to him."

"Where are they?" Shouldn't they be here worrying like the rest of us?

"I haven't told them. I wanted to find out more first. I don't want to worry them for nothing. You know how parents are."

Goddammit! I didn't know how parents were. I could assume my parents would've worried over James and me if anything had happened to us, but now I'd never see it for real. I guessed they would've been in a total freak out when he was kidnapped. "Yeah. I know."

Angelica took a seat, and I wandered to the window and looked out over the parking lot. Not exactly a great view, but better than sitting in a chair staring at everyone's morose faces. How many of the people wandering around down there had just said goodbye to a loved one for the last time? How many were coming to visit a new baby? Tragedy, joy, and hardship were playing out all around us all the time, and I never stopped to notice. How many people were in here suffering all alone? Maybe I could spend some of my spare time visiting patients or even people in nursing homes. Hmm. I'd have to look into that later.

I spoke without turning from the window. "Ma'am, if this is Camilla's doing, will she also be charged with attempted murder?"

"Provided we have proof, yes."

"Who's Camilla?"

Beren answered Sarah's question. "Just someone we're investigating, but don't worry, we'll catch whoever did this."

Anger flared deep in my belly, the kind that begot grudges. I wasn't quick to hold one, but if someone were truly evil, I wouldn't stop till they went down, especially if they hurt someone I cared about. How much did I care about William?

"Lily, please shield your thoughts. I can hear what you're thinking, and I'm sure you don't want me to know everything about you."

My cheeks heated, and I turned around. Ma'am shook her head. "You're not witching too well, dear. You need to be more aware of who's around you and what's going on."

"You're right, but I've just had a shock. Thanks for not wanting to eavesdrop." I reached for the witchy river of power and mumbled the thought-protection ditty. Fine, now I could think in private.

The door opened. James shuffled in, shoulders slumped and dark circles under his eyes. He had the "tired doctor" look down pat. He didn't look well. I hurried over and met him halfway. "Are you okay? You look terrible." My stomach clenched.

He grinned. "I'm tired, but it's because I had to delve quite deep. Camilla is almost the master, or mistress, of burying her secrets, but I'm the absolute master. She'd set a trap in case anyone tried to read Ernest's thoughts. Her magic was all over William. But there's nothing illegal about her protecting Ernest, and she could argue she wasn't targeting anyone, rather just protecting her employee. So we haven't got her yet, but we will. We'll have to figure out a way to crack Ernest's mind or find proof somewhere else. There has to be some."

"How's Will?" Sarah asked.

James took the stethoscope off and handed it to Beren. "He's still out of it. The spell put him to sleep and froze his brain in that state. Beren, you'll have to heal him."

Beren smiled. "Finally, something I'm good at." James handed him the rest of the outfit, and he put it on. "Doctor Beren DuPree reporting for duty."

What the? He was related to Angelica? "How are you two related?" I looked from Beren to Angelica and back.

"She's my favourite aunt, my dad's sister."

How come I didn't know this? I was always the last to know anything. "Oh. Nice to know."

"Well, I'm off. My patient needs me." He winked and turned to leave.

"Good luck," Sarah said.

The door shut after him, and I went back to the window. Waiting was not my strong suit. James joined me and gave me a light shoulder bump. He spoke quietly. "How are you doing?"

I shrugged. "Okay, I guess. I was pretty freaked out at Olivia's. I didn't know what was wrong." I took a deep breath. "I thought he might die, and somehow I feel like it's my fault, even though I know it's not. Maybe if I hadn't been friends with Olivia, this wouldn't have happened."

"That's ridiculous. How do you figure that?"

"If I were the PIB, I would kidnap him, question him under controlled circumstances where I wasn't rushed, wipe his memory, then put him back where I found him." I almost laughed. It sounded like I was talking about a thing or pet rather than a person.

"And this is why you should be working for us full-time."

I shuddered. "Nope. Sorry."

"Well, it was worth a try."

"How's Millicent?" I couldn't believe I was going to have a niece or nephew. I smiled.

"She's still nauseous, but she doesn't vomit every day. I feel so helpless—there's nothing I can do."

"Just make life as easy for her as you can, and if she needs to complain, just listen. I can't imagine what it would be like to feel sick all the time with no way to feel better."

James laughed. "Remember the night I came home drunk from Gordo's sixteenth birthday?"

Oh, God, did I remember. I'd been twelve, and Mum was still alive. "You were so sick. You vomited, which made me vomit, which made you vomit, which made me vomit. Poor Mum. I don't think she got much sleep that night."

"Yeah, the party was fun, though." He sighed. "God, I miss them."

"I know." He put his arm around me, and I leaned against him. "Thanks for looking after me after... everything. You were the best brother ever."

"*Were?* What about now?" He leaned away and regarded me with mock horror on his face.

I giggled. "You're overparenting now. I need a brother, not a father. I'm twenty-four. Please don't be so bossy. I looked after myself for years before I came here. Don't forget that."

"I know. It's just hard to stop myself. I worry about you, Lily. And I feel responsible for bringing you here."

Yes, it had been his fault in a way, but then, it may have happened eventually anyway. "Look, if people are after me here, they would've come to Australia. It's not like there isn't a plane leaving every other hour."

"True, but being involved in PIB stuff probably makes it more dangerous. Today, for instance."

"I wasn't in any danger." I glanced at Sarah, then turned back to James and whispered, "Will William be okay?"

"Beren's the best healer we have. I'm sure he'll have him walking through that door at any moment."

I turned. Sarah had been looking at James and me. She gave me a shy smile. "Sorry. I just... I just hope my brother comes back like yours did. Will told me all about James getting kidnapped. You must've been petrified."

"I was. I'd say James was too, but he was unconscious for most of it."

"I hear you saved him."

"She sure did." James grinned. "I have the best sister ever."

"Aw, shucks." I gave his hand a squeeze, then sat in the chair next to Sarah. "From what James says, Beren will have William back here annoying us in no time."

Sarah laughed. "You know my brother well, I see."

"Ha! Not super well, but well enough to have argued with him a few times. How did you survive growing up with him and not doing him any damage?"

"I have the patience of a saint." She winked. "He's not actually that bad. He's just a worrier, you know? He does have a good heart under that cranky exterior. Also, working away from home mostly, I don't see him that much. That helps." She grinned.

"What do you do for work?"

She hesitated, then said, "I'm a model."

"I knew it! You have that look. You're gorgeous and elegant, even in jeans and a T-shirt. I'm totally jealous, by the way."

"Thanks, Lily. And thanks for being nice about it. Most women give me dagger looks when I tell them. And many of the girls in the catwalk world are insecure—it's hard to make friends. You have no idea how stressful it is when everyone is judging you on looks alone and whether you can fit into size 4 jeans. Most girls look at each other as a threat, someone who'll take their next job from them. Not that I'm complaining. I have a couple of good friends—one's a make-up artist, actually—and it's a dream job if you can get past the superficiality of it. Who doesn't want to get paid for wearing gorgeous clothes and having people fawn all over you?" She laughed.

"Now I'm even more jealous. Sheesh." I grinned.

The door opened, and Beren entered, pushing William in a wheelchair. Relief poured over me. Thank goodness he was okay.

William had dark circles under his eyes, and even Beren walked with less spring in his step than usual, although he was smiling. Sarah jumped up and ran to them. She bent down and threw her arms around William. "Oh my stars! Are you okay? Your eyebrows are singed. What happened?"

"I'm fine. Give me some room."

Sarah stepped back, and William gingerly stood. He walked slowly to a chair and sat.

"You don't look so fine." I shook my head. "What happened with Ernest? He's not a witch too, is he?"

"No, he's not a witch. Camilla definitely booby-trapped his memory. I tried to get in, and there was a flash of light. The next thing I know, I'm here, and my eyebrows suck."

I snorted. "Sorry, you sounded so funny saying it. But seriously, you're probably lucky there wasn't more damage. You could have been badly hurt." My smile faded, the relief of seeing him awake disappeared, and the idea that he could have been killed made me pause. Nausea slid up my throat. It was partly my fault. I should have insisted on being with him, just in case. This wasn't a game, and I'd do well to remember that.

James slid his arm around me. "It's okay, Lily. He knows what he's doing. And this wasn't your fault, so don't blame yourself." Ah, my brother, he knew me so well.

Will stared at me, his cranky expression back. "No, it wasn't your fault. I should've known better, put up a stronger defence spell, just in case, but I got cocky. Never underestimate your opponent. First rule of PIB."

"Is the second rule not to talk about PIB?" We both smiled, and James laughed. "Sorry, I joke around when I'm stressed. It's my go-to thing."

"What are you talking about?" asked Beren. "You're always joking around. I don't think you know how to be anything else."

"Yeah, you're probably right. So, now what happens?"

Angelica, who had quietly observed our reunion, stood. "William, James, and Beren, I want you to have tomorrow off. We all need to regroup and think about our next move. Once we've done that, we'll have a meeting and decide what we're going to do. Sarah, feel free to take William home, and make sure he rests."

"I'll do that. Thanks, Angelica. Once I tell Mum what happened, he'll be trapped on the couch with never-ending bowls of soup." She smirked, and William scowled. Sarah pushed the wheelchair to her brother. "Sit. And I don't want any arguments." Ooh, she could be tough when she wanted. Nice. I didn't feel so sorry for her having to grow up with him now. Seemed like she could hold her own where he was concerned.

Now that things were sorted, I couldn't wait to get out of there. "I should probably call Olivia, let her know William's fine. Also, what happens with Camilla now? Will she know what happened?"

Angelica's poker face was back with a vengeance, and so was her no-nonsense voice. "We can discuss this later, Lily. Let's go." *Yes, Ma'am.* I didn't think saluting was such a good idea, so I hugged James goodbye instead, then followed her out.

"Um, how am I getting home? Didn't you use the toilet?"

She raised her brows. "I did no such thing! It's a cubicle."

"But doesn't it have a toilet in it?"

"Yes, but I didn't touch it." She shuddered. *Potatoe, potahto.*

"I have my wallet. I'll catch an Uber." I wasn't quite sure how I felt, knowing everyone else was witchy enough to travel, but I was useless and had to get home the normal way. Actually, I did know: like a baby in a group of adults. Is that how they all saw me?

"You can't. There's no one watching you. I can travel you back. It's not far, so it won't drain me too much. Then I'll take you to get William's car. You can drive, can't you?"

"Of course. I can even drive a manual. They're cheaper, and that was all I could afford, so I learnt quickly. Sink or swim. Um, will people find it weird that we walk into the bathroom but never come out again?"

"Good that you can drive, and for the other, I'll cast a no-notice spell over us." The lift dinged. "Now, no more discussion." I followed her into the lift, where she mumbled something, the skin on my scalp prickling. We came out on the ground floor and made our way to the bathroom. None of the doctors, nurses, or random people walking past so much as glanced at us. I'd have to learn that one for walking past building sites or groups of drunk guys when I was at the pub, not that I went there much. It was nice to be invisible. As we entered the bathroom, I asked, "How come you don't put a permanent no-notice spell on me, and then no one will have to watch that I don't get kidnapped?"

She checked there was no one in any of the four stalls. "Because other witches can see past a spell like that. It only works for non-witches. Now come in here." She pulled me into the stall at the end with the Out of Order sign on the door. Once locked inside, she mumbled something, and a dark hole, just taller and wider than us, opened up in the wall. "Come on, Lily."

She stepped through, and I followed.

CHAPTER 9

After picking up my equipment and William's car, I set to work editing what few engagement photos I'd taken, and on Tuesday, I saved them onto a memory stick and met Olivia at Costa. The day was warm at twenty degrees, and I braved it in a T-shirt and jeans, although I had a black cardigan tucked into my handbag, just in case. The café smelled divine as usual.

Olivia was at her spot behind the register.

"Hey, Liv. Sorry again about the other day."

"I told you; it's fine." She beamed. "So, what can I get you?"

"The usual, thanks. And I see there's no... difficult customers in today." Camilla was missing, thank God.

"Yes. Today has been awesome, except Ernie went away for work. He left this morning, and he won't be back until Sunday. Some mega investment conference in Dublin."

"Oh. Sounds super exciting. Not." I laughed. "If you're at a loose end, feel free to call me. Maybe we could visit a local castle, and I promise not to vomit." Another thing to feel bad about. Wow, I was wracking things up. But also, Camilla was missing from witch-face duty at Costa, and Ernie was away. *Suspicious much?* And did Olivia not know Camilla was Ernest's boss? She hadn't acted like she'd known her when Camilla was in here being a total witch.

"Ha! You're on." She held her hand out, and I passed her the money and memory stick and stepped to the side to wait for my food. "I'll call you tonight."

"Awesome! Oh, by the way, have you ever met Ernest's boss?"

She frowned. "No. He doesn't like me visiting him at work, because she's really strict about employees doing anything personal during working hours. And he tends to work through his lunch hour. She's a total slave driver, apparently."

"Ah, cool." The next customer was waiting to order, so I stepped away to wait for my coffee.

I focussed on the fact that Olivia was going to call me tonight, and we were hopefully going to visit a castle this weekend. Olivia was so nice. What if I helped break her heart? Gah. Why did life have to suck so much? My order arrived, and I took it to a table at the back—my usual window-seat was taken.

I pushed aside my dilemma—*how unusual, I know*—and savoured my coffee and cake. When I got home later, I called Angelica. "Hi, Ma'am."

"Hello, dear. What is it?" Why did she always sound so unhappy to hear from me? It would be nice to hear some excitement in her voice for a change.

"Camilla's missing from her usual morning harassment of Olivia at Costa, and Ernest supposedly left for a week-long conference this morning."

She left me hanging for a few seconds before answering. "Yes, that's right. We've been watching them. After what happened with William, we added Ernest to our surveillance schedule. I was just going to call you. Everyone else is here having a meeting. I may as well move the meeting to you. We'll be there in a few minutes."

Oh, okay. But why didn't she invite me to the meeting in the first place? She knew I was invested in this case, or maybe that's why she didn't want to tell me. What if I spilled the beans to Olivia by accident? Or what if my personal feelings got in the way and I accidentally-on-purpose ruined something they'd planned? I'd never do that because I believed in right and fair over personal feelings, but Angelica couldn't know that for sure. Plus, there was a first time for everything. Even I had accidents.

I'd just seated myself on one of the Chesterfields when Angelica, James, William, and Beren walked in from the reception room. "Hi. Nice of you to bring the PIB to me."

Beren bowed then sat next to me. "Glad to be of service, Milady." *Nut.* But he was such a nice nut.

James sat on the other side of Beren, and William and Angelica took the Chesterfield opposite. I spoke to William first, because I'd wanted to ask a certain question since the engagement. "How are you feeling?" That wasn't the actual question, but I did want to know how he was feeling. Even though I didn't want to like him, I did. Poor me.

"I'm feeling fine, thanks."

"Great. Also, I'm not sure if you can remember anything from your *discussion* with Ernest, but is he cheating on Olivia willingly, or is Camilla tampering with things?" I held my breath. I did but didn't want to know the answer. If he were cheating on her willingly, he was so going down.

William shook his head. "I can't remember anything, but I don't think I got that far anyway." He blushed. Oh, that was different. He was embarrassed. I shifted and looked at the ground. Argh, I hated awkwardness. The whole room reeked of it as everyone's gazes ducked for cover. It was better if I could tease him or rub him the wrong way and get a reaction, and my mind did not just go there. Nope.

Time to change the subject. "Ma'am, do you know where they went?"

It was her turn to blush. Now I was worried. Something had knocked her poker face off. "They left this morning, and we lost them. Well, our agents lost them. But we checked, and they're not where they said they were going. There is a conference in Dublin, but they're not signed up to attend."

A vortex of rage opened inside me. *That cheating bastard.* But what if he wasn't doing it willingly? Did that mean Camilla could technically be charged with rape? But what if he was in love or lust or whatever with Camilla just because? Gah, my brain couldn't keep up with itself.

"Slow down, Lily." Angelica stared at me.

"Yeah, Lily, your thoughts are even driving me crazy." *Smart arse.* William seemed to have recovered from his embarrassment. I glared at him.

I quickly performed my thought-protection spell. I was so bad at witching. And oh crap, but did he hear that slightly dirty thought I'd had? My cheeks heated. "Okay, so what are you doing about it? How's the investigation going? Is there anything I can do to help?"

James looked at me. "Yes, actually, there is. At this point, Camilla has hidden all the evidence so well that Ernest's memory is all we have left, and she'll know we tried to sift through it. He's in danger. If Camilla doesn't have any feelings for him, or maybe even if she does, she's likely to kill him to save herself. If he dies, his memories die with him."

I swallowed. Crappety crap crap. This was bad. "And you don't know where they are?" My voice rose an octave. What if he were innocent? Even if he wasn't, if he disappeared or was murdered, and Olivia had no answers, she'd spend the rest of her life wondering and pining for him. Just like I had for my parents. "We have to find them."

"Yes, we do." Beren put his hand on mine. "And that's why you're going to help us find them."

"You know I'll do anything."

Beren squeezed my hand. Why was William looking at me like that? Now he was looking at Beren with his cranky face too. I looked down at our hands. Oh. No way! He couldn't be jealous. There I went, reading into shit again, not to mention we had more important things to deal with.

"Do you need me to grab my camera? What are we doing? Where are we going?"

James snorted. "One thing at a time, sis. Just dress comfortable, go to the bathroom, then grab your camera gear, plus a warm jacket. We're going to start with Ernest's apartment this time, but wherever the information takes us is where we're going. We don't have any time to waste. We could be working through the night."

"Is Millicent safe by herself?" She was pregnant, which made her a target of those chasing me, although she wasn't showing, so maybe the bad guys didn't know yet.

"She's staying the night at her parents'." Phew, that was a relief.

Angelica spoke. "The rest of you have things to get, so do it now, and I'll see you back here in ten minutes. Time is of the essence. Let's go." She clapped sharply twice, and everyone disappeared. I didn't think she disappeared them. I was sure they simply had awesome timing. Synchronised witching should totally be in the Olympics.

I ran upstairs to do everything James said, and I was back down in only eight minutes, ready for action. Angelica was waiting for me. "Everyone's going to meet us there. Are you ready?"

"Yep. But is this going to tire you out?"

"No, Lily. I'm one of the strongest witches around. Besides, if I get tired, someone else can help you jump to the next place, providing we need to. We may end up having to grab a car and doing it the non-witch way. Ready?"

"Yes." The black hole opened in front of us, and we

stepped through to a grey-carpeted hallway. The halls were painted light yellow. It looked like a common hallway in an apartment building.

James, William, and Beren were already there, James knocking on a front door. "Open up. Police." They were allowed to lie? I'd have to ask about that later, but I supposed they couldn't just announce they were from the PIB.

No one answered. James nodded. "I'm going in." He placed his palm and ear against the door. Then he pushed the handle down and opened the door. Nifty. No banging and drawing more attention to themselves, plus no bruised or broken shoulders.

We all filed in, the guys spreading out with guns drawn. They disappeared further into the apartment. Angelica stayed with me in the open-plan living area. Dark stained timber floors and creamy-coloured walls gave the room a masculine feel. Two plush faux-suede couches in white lined two walls, and a huge TV hung from another wall. The all-white kitchen opened to the living space. There was way too much white in here. I'd have those couches dirty in a nanosecond if they were in my place.

"All clear," James confirmed as he returned to the living area. "No sign of a struggle, but all his clothes are gone."

My stomach dropped out. "He's done a runner?"

James gave me a sympathetic look, probably realising I was thinking of my friend. "I'd say so. It's not normal to take all your clothes when you go away for a week, is it?"

"Maybe he didn't have much here? You know, like,

maybe he spent a lot of time at Olivia's?" I was trying to be positive. I went into the kitchen and opened the fridge. Milk, butter, cheese and a bottle of wine confirmed he'd at least been here some of the time. But the food couldn't tell me when he was coming back. Stupid silent food. "Ah, I have a question. If he's in because he wants to be, and he knows she's a witch, if you read his mind, won't he die?"

James shook his head. "No, because we're witches, but if he told Olivia, yes, unless Camilla didn't swear him in, and who knows, she may not have, but I doubt it. If people find out we exist, there's sure to be calls for us to be burnt, locked up, or studied. Nothing good can come of it. The select few in government who know have been sworn to secrecy, and it suits them because we help solve crimes, even non-witch ones when they're desperate."

"Okay, thanks."

"Can you take some photos, dear? I'm going to check for magic signatures." Angelica slowly wandered around the living room, seeking, and James turned and went back down the hallway to where I assumed the bedrooms and bathroom were. I took my camera out of my bag, turned it on, and put the lens cap in my pocket. Time to get down to business.

I had to be careful what I thought about, because I didn't want to get any porno shots of Ernest and Camilla, or Ernest and Olivia for that matter. I whispered, "Show me travel tickets," and focussed on the dining table, then the kitchen benchtops. Nothing. Time to visit the bedrooms. The guest bedroom was set up as a study, with a glass and steel table and black office chair. I concentrated on the table. The neat tabletop remained empty. "Show me confirmed travel details on an electronic device."

An open laptop and printer appeared on the table. Ernest sat on the office chair and was leaning over, about to grab a piece of paper that had just popped out of the printer. I snapped the screen and the piece of paper then checked what it was. I zoomed in on the photos on my screen. Damn. The date was from a year and a half ago. I'd keep them, just in case they proved anything else, but they may have been for a getaway with Olivia.

"Show me the most recent confirmed travel details on paper or electronic device that were made from this apartment." Nothing appeared, so I made my way to the next bedroom, where Beren was going through a chest of drawers, and William was checking out the contents of a built-in wardrobe. Standing next to the bed, fully clothed—thank goodness—was in-the-past Ernest. He had his mobile phone up to his ear while he looked at a piece of paper. His grin looked too damned happy. I walked over to him and snapped shots of the paper. I tried to get a look at the phone screen, to see who he was talking to, but it was too close to his ear.

I lowered the camera, switched to play, and zoomed in on the image on the screen. A plane ticket dated today, first class to Paris, but the name on the ticket was Arnauld Frazer. Did Ernest have an alias? If so, which name was really his? The flight had left two hours ago. Time was of the essence, but I needed to ask one question first, and I hoped Camilla's magic didn't interfere.

I stood in the doorway to the bedroom, held my camera up with my eyes shut, and said, "Show me the woman Ernest loves." *Please be Olivia. Please.* I didn't really want to know, but we needed to.

My heart raced as I opened my eyes. I bit my bottom lip. So that was it then. Camilla straddled Ernest on the bed. Was it hot in here? I resisted the urge to fan myself. That was the second time this month. Maybe I should just buy myself a hand fan.

Camilla and Ernest were both naked, and you didn't need a degree in reproduction to know what they were doing. I blushed, then went to the wall at the head of the bed so I could see her face because who knew, maybe Olivia liked to wear blond wigs. But, nope. Camilla's ecstatic face gazed lovingly down, past her sickeningly perky boobs, at Ernest, or Arnauld, or whoever the hell he was. Arsehole was what he was, and that was going to be my name for him from now on. Bastard.

I shivered. This was awkward as hell. I felt like a perv, but at least I had the information I needed. I took one photo from the side of the bed, just in case I needed to prove this to Angelica. Lowering the camera, I went to the doorway and called out. "Ma'am. I know where they are. They flew to Paris this morning. Their plane left two hours ago." Angelica and James hurried into the hallway, and I felt the reassuring presence of Beren and William behind me. "He's travelling under an alias I think. Here." I brought up the plane-ticket picture and handed it to Ma'am.

James looked at the camera over Ma'am's shoulder. "You've done it again, sis. Great work. Looks like we're off to Paris."

I knew it was a case, but oh my God, Paris! I'd always wanted to go. Just thinking about French pastries made my mouth water. "Do I get to come? I mean, is it going to be hard to transport me?"

"I'll spot you this time. Just let me lock up first." James squeezed past Angelica and walked through to the living area.

"Did anyone find anything else?" Angelica asked.

"I found this in a secret compartment in the bottom of a drawer."

I turned around. William stood just behind me, to my right. Entirely too close. I could almost feel the heat radiating from him. Yep, it was definitely hot in here. He waved a blue manila folder.

"Can you just wave that over here for a bit?" I pointed to my face.

He gave me a you're-an-idiot look and turned to Angelica. "I haven't had a chance to look through it all yet, but maybe Ernest wasn't as gullible as we thought. This looks to be records linking Camilla to some of it."

He handed it to Angelica, who leafed through it and smiled. "I think we've finally got her on something. I'm sending this to evidence." It was there, then it wasn't.

I sighed. *Goodbye fan that never was. What a waste.* "Um,

there's something else." Stupid hot cheeks. I needed to warn them that I thought Ernest was on Camilla's side willingly. I'm pretty sure it changed how they would approach everything. If he was on her side, maybe he was gone for good, with her. If he wasn't with her willingly, she would be more likely to off him before we found them. "Scroll to the last photo. I asked the universe to show me who Ernest was in love with."

"The universe?" William smirked.

I folded my arms. "Well, smarty pants, what would you call it? My magic, *the* magic, the gods, what?" He shrugged. "Wow, great answer. Genius."

"Now, now, children, behave. We're heading off to the city of love. Maybe that'll make you act in a more charitable manner towards each other." Beren grinned. We both glared at him.

"We ready?" James was back in the hallway.

"Not yet. Lily said there's one more photo we need to see." Angelica held up the camera.

"Well, on second thoughts, maybe you don't need to *see* the photo. Just take my word for it. Ernest loves Camilla willingly. I mean, I asked the universe"—I narrowed my eyes at William, daring him to open his mouth—"to show me who Ernest really loved. If she'd influenced him magically, that wouldn't be his truth, would it?"

"No, it wouldn't." Great, Angelica had just confirmed this was really it. He was cheating on my friend. My heart broke for Olivia. How would she find out? It couldn't be from me. I wasn't looking forward to the time it would take her to discover he was gone. It would be like waiting for a bomb to go off. Nausea filtered up my throat, making my mouth water.

"Oh!" Angelica's cheeks were bright red. Oh, crap. She'd seen the photo. William took the camera from her. Prickles of heat assaulted my back. He and Beren stared at the screen. William's eyes widened, and Beren's mouth dropped open. Well, this was awkward, and it was all my fault.

William's heated gaze met mine. He cleared his throat then turned to my brother. "James, your sister's trying to corrupt us. I feel violated."

Beren tried not to laugh, but it burst out from between his clenched lips. "Oh my God. You should see your face, Lily. Classic. You're redder than a baboon's bum." Ugliest analogy ever. Thanks. I was sweating too. I finally gave in and fanned my face with my hand. Kill me now, or beam me up. Something… *anything* to get me out of here.

"That's enough!" Angelica grabbed the camera, turned it off, and handed it to me. "We have to go, and next time, Lily, a bit of warning would be nice."

"But I—" Her raised hand cut me off. *I had tried, dammit!*

Beren shook his head, but his grin ruined the chastisement, and William waggled his finger at me.

"James, can we go now?" The sooner we got out of here the better; otherwise, I was going to spontaneously combust from embarrassment.

He laughed. "Yes, dear sister. Follow me." A black hole opened up in the hallway.

I followed him through… to a stinky men's toilet. I obviously hadn't thought things through properly. I should've gone with Angelica. That's what happened when I was distracted—bad decisions ensued.

He hurried us out, past three men using the urinal. I gagged and rushed out into… an airport. Oh my God, I was in Paris! Even if we were just in the airport, we were still here. I grabbed James's arm. "We're really in Paris?" Travellers pulling wheeled suitcases hurried past.

"Yes, Lily. This is Charles De Gaul Airport." He smiled.

"Can we visit the Eiffel Tower and Monet's museum?"

He looked at me like I was stupid. "We're in the middle of an investigation. This isn't a holiday." Why couldn't my brain focus on just one thing without getting distracted?

A message came over the loudspeaker in French, then English. "British Airways flight BA 8752 is now boarding. Last call for passengers, Miss Smith and Mr Bergerac."

It sure sounded like we were on holidays. I resisted the urge to pout. "Okay, don't remind me." My life had been anything but a holiday since I'd arrived in the UK, and it seemed like the fun times were never going to end. It wasn't like I was supposed to be working for the PIB full-time, but I was under contract right now. Maybe once this whole thing was over, I'd hop on the train and have a few days here. That sounded like a plan. Maybe Olivia would need a holiday to forget about everything she didn't know about yet. Yes, that made total sense.

Beren and William had followed us out soon after we

arrived, and now Angelica joined us. "Now what?" I asked Angelica.

"I'll need you to take some photographs. Since we can assume he took all his clothes, he would have checked baggage. We'll concentrate on the carousel where he would've collected his bag."

"But we can't access that area." Unless they had an invisibility spell or a cubicle back there, I wasn't sure how we'd get in. Security was tight these days, and I had a feeling the no-notice spell wouldn't cut it, especially since there were cameras everywhere, and we'd be sure to be chased down later.

"We have a landing place back there," Angelica explained.

"You mean another toilet cubicle?" Why sugarcoat it?

She threw me a stern look. "Come on. I'll take you this time. We're not jumping far."

She mumbled a few words, probably a no-notice spell, hustled me into the women's toilet and into a door at the end. We went in one cubicle and came out another. We exited the toilets. Angelica took stock of the gates we walked past. We turned left again. A couple of minutes later, we came to the baggage-claim carousel. Angelica whispered, "Pretend you're taking photos of me. Cover the whole area. Once we confirm he was here, we can go back out and see if we can track where he went next. He either got a hire car or jumped into a taxi."

This whole thing was a bit like finding a needle in a haystack. My photography wasn't always that accurate, and a city was a big place to try and find someone when you had no idea where they were. What if they had an apartment here and weren't staying in a hotel? They could be anywhere. What if they'd hired a car and driven out of Paris?

"Could Camilla be leading us on a wild goose chase?"

"She could be, but she doesn't know what your talent is, and she hasn't left any other clues, so she's not expecting us to get this far. Let's not stand around too long. We'll look suspicious."

Angelica approached the carousel and mingled with the crowd, pretending she was looking for a bag. I stood back with my camera. "Show me Ernest from today." I scanned the crowd that appeared, clicking as I panned across the room. If only the video function worked with my powers. I'd tried a few times, but it never switched to the other reality. I guess it would have taken too much magical power to leave more than a static image behind.

So many people, all crowded together, and three of them ghostly—one older lady with short grey hair, an older man, and a slim forty-something-year-old woman wearing a pretty printed scarf on her head. Maybe she had cancer. That was so sad. Although, I didn't know for sure they would die.

I shrugged off my unease and walked closer to the herd of travellers, looking for Ernest's familiar face. I slammed into someone.

"Merde! Regardez ou vous allez." I lowered my camera to an angry sixty-something-year-old French man, his beret askew on his bald head. Generalisations were there for a reason. Some French people really did wear berets.

"Sorry! Pardon." I said "pardon" in what I hoped was an authentic French accent. I had no idea what he'd said. The only French I knew was what I'd learned in early high-school French, which is to say, hardly anything.

He looked to the ceiling and mumbled something, then walked off.

Oops. I needed to remember the real world was different from what I saw with my camera. I repeated my request to the universe and lifted my camera, careful not to run into anyone this time when I wandered around. The scene had changed, although I recognised some of the people and clothes from the last image. *Was that? Yes! Click, click.* I carefully picked my way through the travellers to the outskirts of the press of people. One more click and I was done. I put my camera in my bag and grabbed Angelica.

"I got it. Let's go to the car-rental booths." This had been easier than I thought it was going to be. Looked like the universe and I were in tune now. Angelica and I meandered back to the toilet, travelled, then found the guys.

"Any luck?" James asked.

I nodded. "He picked up two checked suitcases. I'm going to see what I can find at the car-rental places."

There they were, not far from an exit, a row of desks. I peered through my camera. "Show me Ernest from this morning." I swept the camera back and forth a few times. Apparently, he hadn't hired a car. I lowered my camera and shook my head. "Time to head outside." Everyone followed me.

Outside, cars zipped past, driving on the wrong side of the road. Yikes. I was likely to look the wrong way and get squished. Note to self: don't rush across the road over here.

Everyone who walked past was dressed elegantly, unless it was me being influenced by the fact I was in Paris. A young woman wore a bright-red T-shirt with an image of a poodle on the front, and a white miniskirt only just covered the tops of her sexy thighs. Large white-framed glasses covered more than half her face, and her lips were painted the same crimson shade as her T-shirt. She sauntered along on white sandal high heels wheeling a small hard-case carryon. How did she walk so fast wearing those heels? The guys watched her as she passed, her slim hips swinging from side to side, side to side. It was kind of mesmerising. I shook my head.

Angelica clapped her hands together twice, the loud cracks putting the traffic noise to shame. I cringed. Was that the loudest clap ever? My ears rang. James looked guiltily at her, although Beren and William just shrugged. I guess they weren't married so they could look at whatever they wanted. And it didn't make me jealous. Not. At. All. Ah, the lies we tell ourselves.

"Gee, there's a lot of footpath to cover." There was more than one exit. I repeated my request to the universe and checked out the area around each exit. At the last one, there he was, getting into a taxi. I made sure to snap the number plate and the driver's ID in the bottom left-hand side of the windshield. I had to zoom in on the ID, because I couldn't get too close to the phantom taxi or I'd hit the vehicle that was occupying the same spot in real time. Done.

We'd been running around all afternoon, and my feet were aching. I could've done with having a seat. This hopping from toilet to toilet didn't allow for rest periods while travelling, and I wasn't used to using my magic so much.

"I'm just going to the bathroom while you decide what we're doing. And can I just say, I could do with a bit of a rest. I'm pooped."

James looked at me. "You do look tired. Not used to your magic yet?"

"Not really." I yawned, and then James and Beren did too. I grinned. "Sorry, made you yawn."

James smiled. "I'll come with you."

"I can go to the toilet by myself. Sheesh."

He came closer and lowered his voice. "You're not safe anywhere, Lily. Just because we're in Paris, doesn't mean we haven't been tracked or followed. Okay."

"Oh, yeah. Okay. I forgot." How did life get so complicated? He escorted me to the bathroom and waited for me outside. Thank God he didn't insist on coming in.

There was a commotion on the way back to the exit. People circled around something. There was shouting, and one woman had her hands in front of her mouth, and she was crying. A man and woman hurried their young son past. I shared a glance with James, and we cautiously approached. I looked over the shoulder of one of the people observing.

An old woman lay on the ground, unconscious. Her glasses lay on the ground beside her, and a young man was performing CPR. I sucked in a quick breath and slapped my hand to my mouth. It was suddenly chilly, and goose bumps spread across my scalp and arms. A tear slid down my cheek. Damn.

I stepped back. James was still watching, so I grabbed his arm and pulled him towards the entrance. He was about to say something but then shut his mouth. Maybe I looked as pale as I felt. Once we were outside and clear of the action, I stopped and bent at the waist. Resting my palms on my thighs, I took some deep breaths. I told James about the photos between breaths. "Have a look on my camera. She was ghostly. I'm sure it was her. I was hoping I couldn't really see that someone was going to die, but I can."

I straightened. James took the camera from Angelica and turned it on. He showed me the screen and flicked through the images.

"Stop. That's the one." I sniffled. Yep, that was the same lady. Even though she was faded, you could tell it was her hair, and she was the only one in the airport wearing pink trousers. Her face wasn't clear enough to be sure, but the rest proved it.

James blew out a huge breath and enveloped me in a hug. "I'm sorry, Lil." I shrugged. What could anyone say? It was what it was.

"What happened?" Beren had moved next to me. James explained what we'd seen. "Oh." That about summed it up.

William clapped James on the back. "Why don't Beren and I catch a cab with Lily while you and Ma'am check out the taxi records? We'll meet you at Castel Café. The view of the Eiffel Tower should cheer Lily up." He smiled at me. "Come on. We'll have a coffee and get going again."

I stepped away from James, who handed me the camera. I put it in my bag and waved goodbye. James and Angelica headed back into the airport, no doubt to find a cubicle while we jumped into a taxi. Being nestled between two hunky Englishmen wasn't the worst thing that could've happened. I relaxed and settled back into my seat.

"Thanks, guys."

"Our pleasure." Beren gently shoulder bumped me.

My gaze was glued out the windscreen the whole time as I soaked Paris in. This was surreal. Pretty apartment buildings with ornate façades and iron lacework balcony railings lined the streets. Rows of plane trees created avenues of green. I even spotted someone walking a giant poodle. So cool!

William shifted, and I was sure I could feel him staring at me. *Don't look. Don't look.*

I had no self-control.

I turned my head. Our gazes met. It was like plunging down a roller coaster. I was falling, and my weightless heart was at risk of floating out of the atmosphere.

His pupils dilated, and his blue-grey irises darkened, reminding me of the ocean on a stormy day. Deep and dangerous. I think it was my new favourite colour. He kept staring, but I chickened out and jerked my head forward. My cheeks heated as I pretended I hadn't just flirted with him. Pretty lame flirting, but I was sure staring into someone's eyes for longer than two seconds meant you were interested. *Don't go there.* It was bound to end badly, as in me falling for him big time, and him having one night of fun, then trying to avoid me for eternity. Plus, James wouldn't be impressed.

Hopefully Beren was oblivious to our little moment. The cab pulled into a side street and stopped near the corner. "We're here." Beren leaned forward and handed the driver a credit card. William got out and held the door for me.

"Thanks." I avoided looking into his eyes this time and took in the Parisian city instead.

Holy cow, the Eiffel Tower was right there, at the end of the street! My mouth dropped open, and I reached for my camera. The tower's golden spire rose above tall green plane trees, shining against a backdrop of blue sky and smattering of white clouds. The staunch yet elegant beauty stood proudly. I snapped a few frames and then headed towards it.

"Hey, Lily. Wait. Where are you going?" Beren ran over and stood in front of me, blocking my way. Oops. Sometimes I got carried away. And let's face it: I was in Paris, and the Eiffel Tower was within spitting distance. As if I wasn't going to get carried away. My subconscious was obviously trying to let me sneak without making me feel guilty.

"Are you sure I can't just go visit for a little bit?" I stared longingly at the icon. So close yet so far.

He shook his head. "We're on the job. Maybe I could bring you back when this case is done. Sorry, Lily."

William stood on the corner watching us, his arms folded.

My shoulders sagged, and I put the camera back in my bag. No one could say I hadn't tried. "I'll be back later, Eiffie."

"Eiffie?" Beren shook his head. "Come on."

Castel Café stood on the corner, maroon awning over the footpath and about six levels of units above. All the café's outside chairs and tables were occupied, so we wandered into the dimly lit interior.

Divine aromas of garlic and coffee with an underlying hint of natural gas permeated the café. Come to think of it, that hint of natural gas was in many of the older buildings I'd been into. It was almost synonymous with Europe for me now. Interesting. I remembered it from our time in Italy.

Beren sat at one of the only empty tables, which was in the middle of the room. French and English conversation intermingled, as both tourists and residents chatted and enjoyed the fare. Rustic orange light shades with prints of French buildings hung throughout the café, and a bar with shiny glasses dangling from racks took up one side of the place. A black-shirted bartender filled a glass stein with beer.

I hung my bag from the chair back and sat.

"What would you like, Lily?" Beren handed me the menu.

Everything was listed in French and English, although I

probably could've guessed most of the French. "I'll have a cappuccino."

"Tell us something we don't know." William smiled.

"Yeah, yeah, but what if I don't say it and I end up with none. I can't risk that." I eyed the food a waiter had just put on a nearby table. Saliva exploded into my mouth. Oh my God. "Lemon meringue pie."

Beren turned to see what I was looking at. "Mmm, that looks good. I think I'll get one too."

I turned to William. "What are you having?"

"Cappuccino and custard tart sounds good."

"Nice choice." I shut the menu and tried to catch the waiter's gaze. He came over and took our order. His French accent was divine. I absolutely had a thing for accents. I hoped nobody noticed me drooling. After he left, I spoke quietly. "How long do you think they'll be?"

William shrugged. "Hopefully not long. James can nudge them with some suggestions. They'll have no problem getting the information."

"I thought it was illegal to do that?" Isn't that what Angelica told me when I'd first arrived?

"There are varying degrees of it. It's frowned upon but not always illegal. Forcing someone to do something that goes against their normal behaviour or beliefs is illegal, but when it's done during an investigation, it's legal. If you were to try and put a suggestion into my head to plant a flower, well, that's hardly damaging to anyone, so you probably wouldn't get into trouble, but if you tried to plant the suggestion to kill someone or for me to give you all my money, well, if we caught you, you'd go to jail. I wouldn't worry, though, Lily, as it's a super hard skill to learn, and there are only a few witches who have the natural talent to get away with it. James is one, but I don't sense that's part of your skill set."

"I hate manipulation and dishonesty, so even if I were capable, I wouldn't want to use it. James isn't like that either, so I'm sure he only uses his powers for good."

"That he does," said Beren. "Your talent is amazing, though, Lily. You don't need any others to be super awesome."

"Aw, shucks. But some of my talent sucks. That lady today." I frowned. I wish I didn't have *that* talent. "I'd call that one more of a hindrance. What's the point of knowing that kind of thing when I can't do anything about it?"

"How do you know you can't do anything about it?" William levelled a serious look my way. "Maybe you have the power to change the future for some people?" Did I? Could I maybe one day? I'd just add that to my to-do list, which was constantly growing rather than shrinking.

"What's your talent, Beren?"

"Healing, but the converse of that is that I'm good at hurting people too. Will and I both have that talent. Not something to be proud of."

William looked at Beren, frustration evident on his face. "We didn't choose this, but we do the best we can with it, don't we?"

Beren blew out a breath. "Yeah, yeah, I know."

Well, this wasn't a conversation I expected to get into. I

didn't like seeing them unhappy or at odds—they were best buddies. "From what I've seen, you're both amazing people doing the right thing. Thanks for keeping me safe." I wasn't sure, but when they watched out for me, they weren't always getting paid. I think some of the time was covered by the PIB, but some of it was as a favour to James and Angelica. Now I felt bad. I'd have to figure out a way they didn't have to watch me so much, or maybe I could invite them to do things with me, but maybe they'd think I was being too forward. And what if they didn't want to hang out with me on a social level?

Happy days! Our food arrived. I slid my spoon through the fluffy meringue then creamy lemon curd. I put it in my mouth and shut my eyes, the tangy sweetness enchanting my taste buds. "Mmmmmm." I groaned. "Oh God, that's good." I opened my eyes. William and Beren both stared at me, their expressions frozen, like they were afraid to move. Then William looked at my mouth. Oh. "You're kidding me, right? This cake is so good, as if I wasn't going to react like that. Try yours." Seriously, this was not *When Harry Met Sally*. Not even close.

Beren grinned sheepishly. William cleared his throat and took a gulp of coffee. Oh, that reminded me. I washed my pie down with coffee but was careful to avoid any accidentally sexy noises or facial expressions. Eating with them was no fun if I couldn't bask in the deliciousness like a pig rolling in mud. Maybe I'd just warn them to look away next time and block their ears.

We'd almost finished eating when James and Angelica

entered the café. James wore a cocky grin, and Ma'am was poker face personified. I could do with some good news, although, I still hadn't figured out how I was going to keep what I knew from Olivia. If she found out I'd had anything to do with arresting her fiancé, she was going to hate me. *Gah, push it away and worry about it if and when it happens, Lily.*

I swallowed the last mouthful of coffee. William stood and made his way to the register. Yay, the PIB was going to get the bill. At least they were good for something other than arresting people. Apparently I was still upset about my incarceration.

"Ready to go?" asked James.

"Yep. The coffee break was just what I needed."

"Good. We also got what we needed, and now it's time to go visiting." James led us outside and down the street to a taxi. He held the door open for me.

"Where's the driver?"

My brother looked around, then pointed at himself with a "surprise" expression on his face. "You're looking at him. We convinced the taxi company to lend it to us. We'll drive it back before we leave Paris. Don't worry."

"Why aren't we just *travelling*?"

"We may need to go to more than one place, and there aren't always public toilets nearby. This will be easier and less tiring. Plus, if we need to, we can leave you safely in the car."

"Oh." I wasn't sure how I felt about that. I wasn't an agent, and there were things I didn't need to see, plus, in a shoot-out—gun or spell—I would probably be a liability.

But did I want to watch my brother and friends run towards danger while I waited somewhere twiddling my thumbs? Where did that saying come from, anyway? I didn't think I'd ever seen someone do that. I certainly hadn't ever twiddled my thumbs. As everyone else piled into the car—okay, Angelica gracefully slid into the front passenger seat—I laced my fingers together and got in some twiddling practice.

The taxi wasn't huge. I'd gotten one window seat, and Beren sat between William and me, the guys' broad shoulders jammed together. The image of a clown car came to mind, and I snorted.

"What's so funny?" asked Beren.

"Mmm, nothing."

He gave me a stern side-eyed glare then gave up. Well, that'd been easy.

I tapped James on the shoulder. "Where are we going?"

"We got an address for an apartment in the 6th Arrondissement. It's practically around the corner."

"Why didn't we just walk?"

"Because"—Angelica turned and spoke to me—"if Camilla manages to escape the conventional way, we have to be able to chase her."

"Why wouldn't she just pop away?" Surely if you had magic, you were going to use it for everything you could.

"She might be exhausted. She's been using her magic a lot lately. Who knows how tired she is? Also, we all need to be fresh to deal with her. We really have to get you travel capable, Lily."

"Yes, Ma'am." The comment stung, another reminder that I was virtually a baby witch, but if I could travel, I could pop over to Paris whenever I wanted, stay for coffee, and go home again. No massive plans would have to be made or time taken.

In a couple of minutes, James double-parked outside a traditional Parisian six-level apartment block. It was one of the ones with the mansard-style grey-slate roofs on the top two floors. "Lily, you'll have to stay here, but I need you to get in the driver's seat, just in case the police come along."

"You're kidding, right? I can't drive on the wrong side of the road. I'll kill someone, probably me. On the upside, William and Beren won't have to follow me everywhere anymore. You guys'll have some spare time to just hang out."

"Oh, don't be so dramatic, dear. Just get into the driver's seat. It's a taxi. You should be fine for a while. We won't be long." Easy for her to say. What if someone wanted me to move the car?

Everyone got out, and I plonked into the front seat. William came around to my side before I shut the door. "Lock the doors, Lily. If anything happens, call me or James. Okay?"

"As in, if I see Camilla or Ernest down here?"

"Ah, yes, that too."

I swallowed. He meant if the bad guys came for me. As he walked away with everyone, a tiny spark of fear ignited in my belly. I locked the doors and looked around, my shoulders knotting, sending pain radiating to the base of my skull.

Great. My indicator was clicking away, yet I tensed at every car that came up behind me, waiting for one to beep and tell me to get moving.

James stood in front of the main doors of one of the blocks lined along the street. He put his palm up to the intercom, and then leaned over to push the door open. Nice work. If that was a witchy trick, how many witches turned to crime for money? Breaking and entering would be so easy if you could just tell the door to open. No wonder the PIB was necessary.

Lime green flashed to my right as a couple ran across the road onto my side of the street. Nice coloured shirt— green was one of my faves. The man wearing the happy shirt reached for the taxi's door handle. My heart sped up. When the door wouldn't open, he bent and cocked his head to the side to stare at me. I shook my head. He pursed his lips and banged on the window. *Sheesh, now I was expected to take fares?* Sorry, but the shirt wasn't enough to sway me. I mouthed "Pardon" and shook my head again. He yelled something in French and lifted his fist at me, although he left his middle finger out of it. Was that ruder? It probably was —a whole fist would be a damn sight more uncomfortable than a finger. *Well, up yours too!* I refrained from sticking my middle finger up, because I didn't want the cab company getting a complaint. Antagonising him wasn't going to help anything. His lady friend pulled his arm until he gave up and went with her.

How were James and the others doing in there? Was Camilla even home? Maybe she and Ernest had gone for a walk or something. A lady in platform stilettos approached my cab—*ha, now it was my cab*. I shook my head at her. She looked confused, then kept walking. There must be a sign on the top of this cab that said I was available, but I couldn't see the controls for it anywhere. Maybe it was a manual thing, and I needed to get out and change it.

I unlocked the door and got out. The little light inside the Taxi Parisien sign brightly mocked me. Great. *How do I turn the damn thing off?* I narrowed my eyes, as if that would solve all my problems. Nope, didn't work. I looked around, although I didn't know why. I didn't think a random person would be able to tell me how to turn it off.

My eyes widened. How hadn't I noticed before? The black van was back, on the other side of the road and down a bit. Crap! I jumped in the taxi and locked the doors, my breath coming fast. I picked my phone up off the passenger seat. Should I call someone? What if they were in the middle of some spell fight and I interrupted at the wrong time and got someone killed?

Was it really *the* black van, or was it a different one? Was I freaking out a bit too hard for no reason? The only way to find out was to get out and check the number plate. Or, I could stay in the taxi and wait for everyone else to get back then get one of them to do it. That would be the safe option, and as much as it chaffed my nerves, I took it.

I had to adjust my side mirror, but eventually, I was able to get it so I could watch the van. Other cars were parked in front of it, so I couldn't see the number plate. Thankfully, there didn't appear to be anyone in it, although with the

darkish tinting, it was hard to tell. It was probably nothing—
a normal Parisian going about their day. Plus, we'd fairly
well established that monobrow and his accomplice were
watching more than attacking, although they had tried to
kidnap me once. Maybe they were just waiting for a better
opportunity. Anger stepped onto the dance floor and
tangoed with fear in my stomach.

Waiting was not my forte, neither was bothering people.
Stuff it. Those crims were not going to rule my life, and I
was not going to sit here shitting myself waiting for something to happen. The van down the street probably
belonged to some hard-working French person, and I was
scared for nothing. Why spend more of my day in fear?

I grabbed my phone and pulled up James's number—
just in case. All I had to do was press the green button. I
gazed out each window before I crawled over the passenger
seat and got out on the footpath side. I locked the taxi and
pocketed the keys. If the taxi were stolen, I'd be in so much
trouble that I'd be better off taking my chances with the van
guys. I hunched over and ran low so I could sneak along
using the parked cars as cover. I ignored the weird looks
passers-by gave me. *Yep, nothing to see here.*

I checked back a couple of times to make sure James
wasn't coming out of the apartment complex. He wouldn't
be happy to find the taxi locked and me gone. I commando-
ran further than the van, as I wanted surprise on my side—
they wouldn't be looking out for me behind their car,
because I was supposed to be in front of them, sitting safely
in my car.

There were lights to cross about fifty metres farther down. I resumed normal posture once the car cover was gone—I was pretty sure that walking like an idiot would make me more noticeable, not less. When the lights changed, I walked as normally as I could. Once across the road, I hid behind a plane tree—Paris was very thoughtful to have planted rows of these things so I could hide my way up the street.

I ducked my head carefully around the tree. The rear of the van was only a few tree trunks away. I wished I could tell if someone was in the van, but it was impossible. Maybe I should just run up to the van, look in and run back to the taxi. In that case, timing was everything. A row of traffic marched down both lanes of the road. Hmm. I ran back to the lights, pressed the walk button, and returned to my tree. That should solve my problem. The light finally turned red, and I ran towards the van. *You are such an idiot.*

My heart raced, and not because of my sprint. I jumped in front of the van, and came face-to-face with… no one. It was empty. Now I was close enough, the disabled parking sticker was obvious on one side of the windscreen—so it wasn't their van. I bent over and checked the number plate. Nope. Not theirs. I sucked in a lungful of air and huffed it out again. I was careful to look both ways, and the right ways, before I crossed the road laughing. *I'm Lily, Queen of the Idiots. Behold my stupidity!*

I was still grinning when I unlocked the taxi and got back in the driver's seat. I locked the doors, put my seatbelt on, and stuck the key back in the ignition. Phew. False alarm. Everything was good. Now I just had my PIB peeps to worry about.

Click.

What was that? It kind of sounded like someone cocking a— Cold, hard metal pressed into the side of my head, just above my ear. I froze.

Crap.

A muffled male voice came from behind the back seat. "Drive."

CHAPTER 10

S weat prickled my forehead and slicked my palms. I hated speaking too soon, saying everything was fine. It was clearly my fault: I should have said, "touch wood." The thing I had going for me was that only a bigger idiot than me would demand I drive in Paris, on the wrong side of the road. The traffic zipped past. Should I warn him? Nah. The only way I was going to get out of this is if I crashed the car, which wasn't going to be hard considering my lack of experience driving on the right—or wrong—side of the road.

I glanced in the rear-view mirror. His face was covered with a black balaclava. I wanted to ask if he was the same guy who'd try to grab me in Westerham, but I was scared to talk, in case it made him want to pull the trigger. Although, if he'd wanted me dead, he would've done it already. Right?

I had to assume whoever had sent him wanted me alive, at least for a while. "I should warn you: I'm a crap driver."

The gun pressed harder against my head. *Okay, you asked for it, buddy.* Operation Crash the Taxi commenced.

I put the left indicator on, checked for cars, then pulled out. Oh, God, I was driving in Paris. I bit my lip and concentrated. Could I crash the car on purpose, or would I chicken out? Also, James and Angelica were going to be so pissed that I'd totalled the taxi. I should never have gotten out to check the van. I'd stuffed up again. When would I learn?

"Turn left here." He waved the gun, bopping me in the cheek.

"Ouch, dumbass. Watch where you poke that thing." Kidnapping me was one thing, but until he killed me, I wasn't going to play nice. He didn't have to be violent. I was driving, wasn't I? I scowled. I was so crashing this taxi. I didn't care if I got hurt doing it. If he got me wherever he wanted me to go, it would be game over for me. Not happening. Also, crap—a left turn was tricky.

"Shut your mouth, bitch." Heavy English accent. Maybe it was one of those guys from the black van. Just because the other van hadn't been theirs, didn't mean they hadn't popped into Paris and snagged another car.

I slowed down, indicator on, and waited for cars coming the other way to pass. If I were in Sydney, a left turn would be one where I hugged the kerb. The cars cleared, and I went. My gaze darted everywhere to look for somewhere safe to crash. Yes, I saw the irony in that statement.

Then I saw my opportunity. I knew I was about to cause all kinds of trouble for James, but if I didn't take this chance, what if I didn't get another one?

The traffic slowed up ahead, but against every instinct, I pushed my foot down harder and accelerated.

"Slow down, you crazy bitch. What are you doing?"

Crashing into a police car, apparently. This is gonna hurt like a—

Bang!

The airbag deployed, smashing me in the face, as metal crunched and glass sprayed everywhere. The moron in my back seat had no belt on, and he went flying through the windscreen. I would have laughed if my face didn't hurt like a witch.

My mobile rang somewhere in the wreckage. But I couldn't see it, and it hurt to move. I hoped no one else was hurt as I squinted my aching eyes and looked out through where the windscreen used to be. The taxi was a mangled disaster, and so was the back of the police car, but their crumple zone had worked, and the rest of it looked fine, oh, except the roof, where the guy who'd tried to kidnap me lay, not moving. Had I killed him? If I hadn't felt nauseous before, I did now. I didn't want to kill anyone, just escape. *Please don't be dead.*

The police lights flashed. Two police got out, one looking slightly dazed. The driver, who looked fine, had his hand on his hip, maybe deciding whether we were terrorists or not. He checked out the guy on his roof then cautiously walked towards me, gun drawn. To be fair, the guy on his roof had a balaclava on. Once the police officer was next to the car, he lowered his gun. Warmth oozed down my face. I touched my temple and cheek. Slimy, wet. Oh, my palm was red. I must be bleeding.

"Est ce que ca va?"

Huh?

High-school French came back to me. "Parlez vous anglais?"

"Yes, miss. What happened?"

"That man was trying to kidnap me. He has a gun." I looked to where the guy was still lying across the roof of the police car, his arms hanging down one side. Sharp pain speared through my head. I groaned. *What did you expect? You just crashed a car.* Oh, that's right, I *had* just crashed a car. It was official: I was definitely loony.

The policeman leaned closer, his brow wrinkling. "Miss. Miss."

My mouth wouldn't form the words to answer. I tried to smile, to say I was okay, but sharp agony cut across my forehead. My eyelids fell shut, and the world disappeared.

❧

I WOKE TO AN ACHING BODY AND HEADACHE. JAMES WAS IN A chair next to my… hospital bed? William sat on a chair next to him, his hair dishevelled, tie askew, and lines creasing his forehead. He sat up straight. "She's awake."

James jumped up and grabbed my hand, blocking my view of Will. I gave him a small smile. "Hey."

"Hey, yourself. What the hell happened? I thought we told you to stay put?"

William stood and put his hand on James's shoulder. "Go easy. Seriously, she just woke up. I'll call Beren." He walked out, his phone to his ear.

"I know you told me to stay put, but I saw a black van. I thought it was the kidnappers from before. I stuffed up. I'm sorry."

"We saw the guy at the crash site. He was dead."

I felt the blood drain from my face, and dizziness witch-slapped me in the head. I shut my eyes and swallowed the nausea.

"It wasn't your fault, Lily."

How could it not be my fault? But I didn't have the energy to argue. It was all I could do to not throw up. A tear heated my cheek, glided down, and dripped off my chin.

Without opening my eyes, I asked, "How did you find me?"

"I've programmed a GPS tracker into your phone. We got there just as they were loading you into an ambulance. I managed to get a look at that guy's face. It was the driver from last time. There were traces of magic around him, so he may not have died from the impact but from failing to carry out his assignment." That didn't make me feel much better. Well, maybe a little.

I risked opening one eye a crack. "What happened with Camilla?"

"Don't ask."

Oh, that well.

The door opened, and Beren and William came in. They both looked worried, but then Beren grinned and came to the bed. He was wearing his doctor getup. "Dr. Beren at your service."

I couldn't help but laugh a little—not too much, because my head still hurt like a witch. "And what is Dr. Beren going to do?"

"I'm going to fix what ails you. Then we're going to get out of here. We've warded your room so anyone thinking to come in decides not to when they get near. Ma'am's already *deleted* your paperwork."

Interesting, but I couldn't think on it because... sore head. God, and what about the taxi stuff?

William appeared next to Beren. "That's been taken care of. Don't worry about it." Oh, my mind shield must have gone down when I crashed the car, which was understandable. Multitasking was hard when you were unconscious. William gave me a small smile. "That it is."

"Can you two stop with the private conversation?" James winked.

"Hey, big bro, it's not my fault you can't read minds." Agony shot through my head, and I winced.

"I think it's time to get you fixed, Lily. Hold still. This will take a couple of minutes. It might hurt a bit, but just hang in there. Okay?" At least he was honest. Beren placed his palms firmly, but not painfully, on either side of my head.

I whispered, "Okay," shut my eyes, and braced myself.

Whatever happened, I doubted it could be as painful as crashing a car.

My skin warmed, and so did my insides. Prickles of pressure burst throughout my head. It ached more than hurt. The sensation gradually moved down my body, leaving non-pain in its wake. When the sensation reached my feet, the warmth faded away.

"I'm done. You should be as healthy as you were before, albeit tired. If you have any pain later, let me know."

I opened my eyes. I touched my face, where there must have been cuts, but the skin was smooth, and my head didn't hurt. Nothing did. I smiled without holding back, and yep, all good. "Thank you, B! You're the best."

His cheeks pinked. "I do what I can. I'm just glad you're okay. You gave us quite a scare, miss. So what actually happened?"

I turned to look at James. Now that I was okay, he probably thought it was fine to be angry. His lips were pressed tightly together, as if he were holding himself back from saying stuff.

Well, might as well get it over with. I told them everything.

William's eyes were wide, his hands balled into tight fists at his sides. "You crashed the car on purpose? I'm not sure if I'm proud of you or I want to strangle you. Was that really necessary?"

I wasn't even angry, just sad. "I know I ruined everything. I really am sorry. But, Will, if he'd gotten me wherever he wanted, you never would have seen me again." I'd known it deep in my gut. Maybe dying in a car crash—I couldn't call it an accident since it was on purpose—would've been the better option than being imprisoned, used, and killed. At least mine and others' secrets would die with me. Whoever wanted me would surely have forced me to use my magic for them—that's what logic told me.

I patted myself down to check I wasn't naked under the hospital gown—phew, bra and undies in place—before I slid my legs to hang over the side of the bed, and sat up. "Where are my clothes?"

James hesitated before he said, "We threw them out. They were bloodied and full of glass shards."

"Oh. Can you magic me something from home?"

William stared at me. "What? You're not upset?"

"They're only clothes. I can buy more. Seems to me jeans are a bit trivial to cry about, don't you? Maybe if I'd been wearing super-expensive designer threads, I'd be worried, but I wasn't. So I'm good with it."

James shut his eyes and mumbled something. My emerald-green turtleneck sweater, a pair of faded blue jeans, and a pair of socks appeared in his hands.

"Nice choice. Thanks." I grabbed the clothes and disappeared into the bathroom. Luckily they'd gotten me a private room, although it wasn't luck. They'd known what they were doing.

I dressed, toileted, and went back out to find my shoes, which were sitting neatly next to a small built-in closet. As I laced them up, I asked, "What happened with Camilla?"

James answered. "We found her apartment, but they

weren't there. We searched the place and were going to wait till they got back, but then I got the weirdest feeling, and I knew you were in trouble, so I tried to call, but you didn't answer. That's when we got out of there and followed the GPS."

"How did you sort out the taxi stuff? Surely they'll freak out when they find out what happened to their vehicle?"

"We used PIB money to buy an identical car, and we magicked the taxi stuff onto it and the same number plate. It took a huge amount of magic, but Angelica and William sent the wreck and the dead body to PIB headquarters, and I wiped the memories of the police and a few bystanders. We also had PIB head office pull some strings with the French PIB. It took a few hours, but the cover-up is complete. That's why Angelica isn't here: she's exhausted. She'll probably sleep until this time tomorrow. William should have gone home too, but he insisted on staying." James shot him a sympathetic look.

"I wanted to make sure your sister was okay. So sue me." He shrugged, so nonchalant. He was totally pulling off the "I don't care that much about Lily" façade, but the fact that he'd stayed spoke volumes.

"Well, thank you all for pulling together to save me. I appreciate it more than you all know. I'm just sorry I stuffed up catching Camilla."

"Don't worry about that," said Beren. "We'll be back on the case in a couple of days. We just have to hope she wants to keep your friend's fiancé around."

I let out a heavy sigh. If Ernest was acting without free

will—and even though my magic said he wasn't, maybe he really was—and Camilla killed him in the next few days, it would all be my fault. Would I ever get the hang of being a witch?

"At least you know where they are now."

James shook his head. "Not necessarily. We disarmed her protection wards to get in, but it's hard to redo someone else's magic the same way. We tried, but she's not stupid. As soon as she got home, she could probably tell something was off. All she had to do was look for other magic, and she would have seen ours. We scrambled it, but she'll probably find somewhere else to run."

Oh. I really had ruined everything. "I think I should stay home next time. I seem to do more harm than good."

William focussed his intense gaze on me. "No. We need you. We never would've found where they were in the first place without your magic. Angelica's already said when you're better, we need you to find out where they went next, but you're going to learn to travel first so we can send you home without dramas when you're done."

I couldn't help the little heart flutter when he'd said, "We need you." Was he secretly saying *he* needed me?

"I'm off. I need sleep. See you all in a couple of days." William vanished without so much as a hug. He obviously didn't *need*, need me. My magic was useful. I guess I should get used to people wanting me for it, even though I couldn't wield it properly. It was time I got my magic act together, so I was less of a liability and more of a badass.

"Thanks again, Dr. Beren." I gave him a hug.

"Any time. See you two at Thursday's meeting."

Then it was just James and me.

"James, how come we can't see other people's doorways?"

"You can only see ones you've been programmed to use. When you create one, your magic automatically includes you. If you want to take someone with you, you have to tell your magic to include them, and then they'll be able to see your doorway."

"Okay. That makes sense." Not much else did, but one thing was better than nothing.

"Ready, Lily?"

I nodded and followed him through the swirling doorway.

CHAPTER 11

Healing and the drama of the day had left me exhausted. I showered and went to bed as soon as I arrived. I would have checked on Angelica, but I didn't want to disturb her—she needed her sleep. It was almost midnight when I got into bed, and I slept until 4:00 p.m. the next day. I woke feeling tired and with dribble running down my chin. Some things never changed.

I dressed and wandered down to the kitchen with my phone. I had two missed calls and a text from Olivia—thankfully, my phone had survived the crash, not like the kidnapper. I still felt bad about it. I knew he was an evil person—because who else would do that—but killing people wasn't my thing. I would carry that with me forever.

I opened the text message.

Tried to call you, but you're not answering. I hope you're okay. Just wanted to see if you wanted to do something on Thursday. Maybe we could check out one of the local castles. Anyway, call me when you can. Liv.

How was I going to act normal around her?

I set up the coffee machine and pressed the button, then poured milk into another cup and stuck it in the microwave for sixty seconds. It was time I used magic to do more things, and I wanted to try it to froth my milk in an instant, but after yesterday and how tired I still felt, I wasn't going to push it. There was always tomorrow to start witching better.

Once I had my coffee, I plonked myself in one of the armchairs next to the fireplace. I took a deep breath and dialled Olivia. She picked up almost immediately. "Lily! Thanks for calling back. I was a bit worried when I couldn't get hold of you."

"I'm fine, just had a bit of a virus or something. I slept most of yesterday and today. I just got up, actually." At this rate, she was going to think I was a sickly person who caught every virus going around. First London, now this.

"Oh, no! I hope you're okay."

"I'll live. So how are you?"

"I'm okay. Missing Ernest. He called last night to say goodnight. He said the conference is boring as hell."

Was he planning to return to Olivia? If he'd run for good, why was he still calling her? Maybe he was hedging his bets. "I bet it is." It would be boring if he were actually at a conference. I bit my tongue. Surely lying would get easier? Yeah, nah. I knew it wouldn't. Would this be my life from now on? Lying to all my friends? Beren had a point when he said to only befriend or fall in love with other witches. I was sure I could do one but maybe not the other. William was a conundrum for another day.

"Do you think you'll be well enough to do something tomorrow?"

"Probably. I think Angelica had some work she wanted me to do, but I'll check with her when she comes in, and I'll let you know. I'm pretty sure her thing won't take too long."

"Awesome. I'll chat to you later."

"Bye."

Was Angelica up yet? Maybe I should check on her. I finished my coffee and went upstairs, to the first floor, where she had her master suite. The door was shut. I didn't want to wake her, but I needed to know she was okay. Hopefully she wouldn't be too angry about yesterday. I knocked.

"Come in."

I opened the door. She was dressed and just putting her shoes on.

"Good afternoon, Ma'am. How are you feeling?"

"Well rested, thank you. And how are you feeling, Miss Disaster?"

I cleared my throat. "I'm a bit tired but fine, thanks." I met her piercing gaze. "I'm very sorry about yesterday. I went against what everyone asked and stuffed everything."

Her expression held no sympathy, but at least she didn't look ready to kill me. "Yes, you did ruin things, and you almost got yourself killed. Do you understand now why you must listen when your brother or I ask something of you?"

"Yes, Ma'am. It's just—"

"Up, up, up." She held her hand high, palm towards me

in the universal gesture for stop... or shut up. "I don't want to hear it. No excuses, Lily. Now, we have work to do. You need to learn how to travel." She marched past me and out the door.

We spent the next four hours getting me travel ready. When we'd finished, Angelica witched the frozen leg of lamb that was in the freezer into a delicious roast with gravy, baked potatoes, and pumpkin. Yum! I slumped into the dining chair and ate. My eyes kept wanting to close. Using magic was hard work. Then I remembered going out with Olivia. "What time is this meeting tomorrow, and do I have to be there?"

"Two in the afternoon, and yes, I want you there. It's at PIB headquarters this time." I looked at her, aghast. "You're going to have to go back there eventually, and after yesterday, you don't deserve any concessions. You disregarded everyone else to do what you wanted, no matter that you gave your brother and I a heart attack, not to mention William and Beren. Those boys care about you, Lily. You let a lot of people down yesterday."

I should've known I'd gotten off too lightly before. Shame heated my cheeks. She actually cared. I wasn't used to being a failure or to having so many people worry about me. As a photographer, I called all the shots, literally, and I'd always made people happy and been successful. Taking orders and considering others was going to take a lot of acclimatisation. I was used to being by myself. With the exception of Sophia and Michelle, my friends in Sydney, I didn't answer to anyone, and even they didn't expect me to consult with them on my day-to-day activities. "I know. All I can say is I'm sorry, and I'll do better next time. It's not always easy for me. My life has changed completely, and I'm still adjusting. I'll try not to let you down again, Ma'am."

"Good. You can travel there by yourself." She slid a piece of paper across the table. "Memorise those coordinates. They'll fade off the paper in two hours. Once you remember the coordinates, you'll need to use a scramble spell on them, so if you forget to renew your mind-shield, no one can get them from your head."

"Why don't I just do that for all my private thoughts?"

"Because it takes a lot of energy, and you have new thoughts every second of every day. Just make sure to use it for any coordinates to private homes or security facilities. To create a ward, imagine a secure box around the number, and say, "No one else must know this number. Scramble it to hide it from those who would plunder.""

I raised my brow. These rhymes were terrible. "Why can't I just say it without the rhyme?"

"It's been specifically designed to include everyone who would read your mind and say exactly what we need with no oversights. Plus, it's easy to remember a terrible rhyme than a convoluted monologue."

She had a point. I read the number over and over, until it was embedded into my memory. Then I said the rhyme. My scalp prickled as I said it, and then it was done. Now I just had to use it without killing myself or chopping a foot off. I wondered if Beren could grow someone a new foot?

"Is it okay if I go to a local castle tomorrow morning

with Olivia? She offered to take me, and she needs the company. She misses Ernest."

"Of course, but don't say anything. Can I trust you?"

"Of course. I know I haven't done everything everyone's asked, but I don't want her to have to take an oath that might get her killed. Is there a way I can get a reminder before I blurt anything out, like if my mouth takes over and goes to say something that hasn't been filtered properly?" My lack of filter often got me into trouble, and that was fine, but I didn't want to drag anyone else down with me.

She smirked. "No, but maybe you could make one up. I'd certainly feel better knowing it was there, and if it works, we can roll it out to the other PIB witches."

Ooh, that would be exciting, if I could make it work. Although, I did doubt my ability to make it happen, but there was no harm in trying… except if I said the wrong thing and wiped out my ability to ever speak again. "Okay. I'll think on it." I looked at the piece of paper one more time, then repeated the numbers quietly before sliding the paper back to Angelica. "I should be good."

Her sceptical expression showed she didn't believe me. Well, we'd both know tomorrow whether my memory could handle it. I crossed my fingers, took my plate to the dishwasher while Angelica magicked everything else away, and then I went to bed. On the way up the stairs, I texted Olivia to tell her we were good to go in the morning.

I fell asleep thinking of new spells.

THE NEXT MORNING, I WOKE TO RAIN THRUMMING AGAINST my dormer window. I dressed then opened the plantation shutters. Sombre dreariness overlaid the sloping rooftops and greenery into the distance, until the view smudged to grey. I would definitely need an umbrella and warm jacket today. So much for it being late spring, although I couldn't be too sad, because back in Sydney, it was almost winter and likely a little bit colder than it was here. I'd definitely have to buy some super warm clothes before winter came. I imagined it would be freaking freezing here compared to winter in Sydney.

I packed my phone, umbrella, wallet, and camera into my knapsack, had a coffee, then waited for Olivia in the living room. My camera had also survived my stupidity, thank God. Although, because of all the work I'd had lately, I did have money to replace it, but spending that money would still hurt. Plus I loved my camera. It went with me everywhere. I didn't want a new one: I wanted this one.

Thanks to Beren's healing, I had no scars on my face. Apparently, I'd had several cuts on my forehead, cheeks, and nose. Apart from not wanting to be scarred, how I would have explained that to Olivia, I had no idea. I'd been thinking of spells so I wouldn't say the wrong thing, and I'd come up with one. Hopefully it wouldn't backfire and leave me unable to answer the door when Olivia came because I'd done something unexplainable, like turned myself into a cat or something. If this worked, I was going to start a book-of-spells diary.

I imagined standing in the golden river of power, its

luminescent water flowing around me. "Filter my thoughts, and only let words form for the ones that won't cause remorse." I flung my arms wide to add some dramatics— everyone was so subtle, but I felt like having some fun. Warmth briefly drifted over my scalp and face. Hmm, I needed to test it with something fairly harmless but slightly upsetting. I'd think of something by the time Olivia turned up.

The sound of crunching gravel and a car engine indicated I'd been optimistic in my assessment. Well, I was sure I'd think of something in the car.

I didn't wait for her to knock and opened the door. I stepped outside and locked it as Olivia was getting out of the car.

"Hey, Liv." I squinted against the raindrops hitting my face.

"Hey, Lily." She ran up and gave me a quick hug. "It's a bit wet."

"Yep, it is. Let's get in the car."

We raced to get out of the drizzle. Once we were safely strapped in, she reversed down the driveway. She turned left, away from the village. "So, where are we going?"

"I thought it would be nice, notwithstanding the weather, to take you to Hever Castle. It's about twenty minutes' drive. The gatehouse dates from about 1270. Anne Boleyn used to live there, and Henry VIII used to visit there all the time."

"Sounds like a happening place." I laughed. "The history sounds so cool. Can't wait to see it!"

"I hope you brought your camera."

"Yep. I hardly go anywhere without it."

"I noticed." She smiled. "Thanks for the photos, by the way. Even though you didn't get to stay for the whole thing, the photos you sent me were incredible. My parents said to say thank you. They're also insisting you keep the deposit."

I looked at her, my mouth open. "They're thanking me for bailing in the middle of things and leaving them with drama on such an important day? I find that hard to believe. They must be two of the most forgiving people ever, and you come a close third. And I want to give the deposit back. I didn't do a proper job."

"No way. The photos you did take were amazing. We won't accept the money back." Her smile fell. "You know how they don't like Ernest? They said it was a bad omen and reminded me I could still call the wedding off."

"Oh." Now I wasn't smiling. I wish I could tell her, but I couldn't, and what would I even say? Maybe now was the time to test out whether my spell worked. I'd never liked his slicked-back hair. I bit my lip then plunged on. "Well, his hair—" My mouth stopped, refused to form words. I opened and tried again. Nothing. My mouth wouldn't even open this time. Not bad.

"His hair, what?"

"His hair is nice and thick." Luckily I hadn't put an anti-lie spell on myself.

"I like it, and the product he uses smells yummy. Sometimes I just lie there and smell his hair."

Thank goodness she was looking at the road, because

while my mouth wouldn't offend, my facial expressions weren't censored, and my current expression was a touch of too much information mixed with a healthy dose of ew.

I relaxed a little once I knew my spell had worked. I couldn't wait to tell Angelica how awesome I was.

"What time do you have to go to work with Angelica?"

"Not till two." I checked the car clock. "It's only nine. We should have plenty of time."

"I don't think I've ever asked, but what does Angelica do?"

I should've expected that question sooner or later. "She's a manager at a secret government facility. I promised I'd help her with some basic office stuff this afternoon. Her secretary's sick."

"Ooh, that sounds cool. What kind of secret government facility?"

"I can't say. I've been sworn to secrecy, and they know where I live." I laughed. Telling her part of the truth would make it easier to deflect questions later. "I had to sign a non-disclosure agreement. If I break it, I'll go to jail."

Her mouth dropped open. "Whoa! That's tough."

"I know. Tell me about it. She doesn't tell me much of what goes on there, so I don't actually have much to spill, thank goodness. Have you heard from Ernest today?" *Why did I have to go there?* I just couldn't help myself, apparently.

"No, but I'm expecting him to call tonight. I can't wait till he gets home. I've missed him."

My brain countered with, *but he's probably never coming home, the bastard.* My mouth behaved and stayed closed.

When everything was over, I hoped we'd still be friends. She'd need a good friend, and while I knew she had some, I wanted to do my part to help her get over him, since I was assisting in uncovering his deceit.

I grinned at the sign that said Hever Castle and squealed a little. I was going to see a real castle! Olivia found a spot and parked. The parking lot was a mud bath, and we squelched our way to buy tickets. My poor hiking boots. At least we both had umbrellas.

Tickets in hand, we set off towards the castle, excitement filling me so I was almost skipping. We passed through a Grecian or ancient Roman style garden on the way to the castle proper—I really needed to brush up on my history. The garden's ancientness was deceiving, as it was apparently created in the early twentieth century. Down the path, through ionic, or were they Doric, columns supporting a stone archway was the slate-grey-yet-slightly-brown lake. It was also created around the early twentieth century by the guy who started the Waldorf Astoria hotel in London. Talk about rich history. This was the stuff I missed in Australia— the old buildings and stories to go with them.

Thunder cracked, and the drizzle turned to a downpour. For convenience sake, my umbrella was one of those fold out ones where you pressed the button and *whoosh*, *click* an umbrella appeared in the form it's supposed to take. Unfortunately, mine didn't have a large *brella* part, and my hair and face were the only things that weren't getting wet. Olivia didn't look much better off.

"I'm running," I said as I took off. Surprisingly, she

followed. I had no idea if she did any regular exercise, but she was no slouch. She kept up with me the whole way. We stopped in front of Hever Castle, panting. I wanted to take photos, but I didn't want to ruin my camera, so I took my phone out and snapped a few with that.

It wasn't the biggest castle, but it was still impressive. Four stories of stone with crenellations around the roof, all surrounded by a moat. The drawbridge was down, a steady stream of visitors crossing it, despite the bad weather. I supposed weather didn't respect sightseeing holidays, so you just had to push through the discomfort.

We crossed the drawbridge and went down a few steps to the central courtyard, framed on all sides by Tudor architecture. "The windows are so pretty!" I took more photos with my phone.

"I know. It's been so well preserved."

We stuck our umbrellas in an umbrella holder in the entry and wandered through. Numerous times, I had to stop myself from taking photos. I didn't want to get pictures of something I couldn't explain, plus it would definitely freak me out if I snapped a picture of Henry or Anne. Too weird. I'd wanted to block my magic, but then I might have said something and put Olivia in danger. Priorities.

The first room we came upon was a ginormous yet cosy sitting room, furnished with cream-coloured lounges, timber-framed chairs, and Persian rugs over a polished timber floor. There was even a grand piano in the far corner. The room screamed decadence, from the decorative plaster ceilings to the ornate timber panels lining the walls. It smelled of old books and ancient dust.

Olivia's phone rang. She pulled it out of her bag and checked the screen. "It's Ernest!" Her face lit up, and she answered it. "Hey, honey. How's it going?" She nodded while he spoke. "I'm just at Hever Castle. Yeah, it's pouring at the moment." He said something else I couldn't make out, but his voice projected enough to hear he was talking. "Another couple of hours. Then I'll head home. Okay, enjoy your conference. Chat to you later. Love you." She dropped her phone back in her bag and grinned.

"Happy much?" I smiled and hoped it didn't look like a grimace.

"Very." She bit her lip. "I've been feeling kind of weird lately, like something's got him distracted. He's not as doting as he was before. I'm pretty sure there's nothing to it. I'm probably just being paranoid." A small nervous laugh tittered out. If ever I were to say something, now would be the time. But I couldn't. She'd still be unlikely to believe me, and how would I explain why I thought what I thought?

A prickly tingle crept down my back, and I shivered. We moved back through the entry foyer and to the dining room, where a sixteen-seat dining table took centre stage, and guild-framed portraits hung on the timber-panelled walls. So much dark timber made the room feel oppressive, coupled with the small windows that only let in a trickle of low light, and I wanted to escape outside.

Olivia led me to a staircase. As we neared the top, I had the sensation someone was behind me. I looked back, but no one was there. *Stop being paranoid, Lily.* We walked through to a study. There wasn't anyone else around, so I shook off my unease. The castle was quite lovely, and it annoyed me that I was creeped out. I wanted to enjoy the morning with my friend, finally doing something fun. I walked to one of the walls and read a plaque while Olivia looked at a display against another wall.

There was that damn tingling again. I reached my hand around awkwardly and scratched my back, but I couldn't reach all the way down to the middle of my spine. Maybe coming here had been a bad idea. What if whoever wanted me had sent new guys already? And if they cornered me here, there would be no way whoever was watching me today would get here in time. I hadn't noticed Beren or William skulking around behind me, so I had to assume the PIB had sent agents I didn't recognise.

I'd almost reached the itch in the middle of my back, when my scalp went nuts. It was like a thousand lice were holding a dance party in my hair. I shook my head and scratched.

An intake of breath came from the other side of the small room. I spun around.

Camilla!

She had Olivia in a headlock, her palm to her forehead. A flash of light burst from Camilla's hand, and Olivia slumped in her arms. Camilla looked up at me, grinned, and stepped backwards, dragging my friend with her.

They both vanished. Mega crap! She must have taken her through a doorway. I ran to the spot where they'd disappeared. There was nothing left but the last dull vibrations of recently used magic. My breath came faster. I frantically looked around for help, but the room was empty, and even if someone had been here, what could a non-witch do except freak the hell out at what they'd just witnessed?

I fumbled through my bag, grabbed my phone in clumsy fingers, dropped it, then found it again. I dumped my bag on the floor and dialled Angelica. She picked up on the second ring, thank God. My thoughts were racing. I needed to go after Camilla. Now. "Ma'am, they've taken Olivia."

"Who, Lily?"

"Camilla. Ernest called Olivia a few minutes ago and asked where she was. It must have been so his girlfriend could make a doorway and take her. She appeared from nowhere, zapped Olivia in the head to make her unconscious and snatched her. I thought witches couldn't just pop in anywhere."

"Maybe your friend told her fiancé where she was bringing you today, and Camilla popped into a public toilet nearby and set up a doorway point last night. Are you still there?"

"Of course I am. Where else would I be?"

"Don't be smart with me, dear. Do you remember the PIB coordinates?"

"Yes, of course. You want me to come there now?" Okay, so I wasn't sure if I remembered, but I was going to trust my brain this time, which wasn't always the smartest thing to do.

"Yes. I'll bring the meeting forward. But before you do, I want you to set some landing coordinates for me."

Okaaaay. I'd just learnt to travel and now she wanted me to do something new? Good luck with this working out. "I'll try. What do I have to do?"

"Draw from the power and pull up the world map in your mind."

We'd practiced that at her place when she'd taught me how to travel. I did what she asked and zoomed in on the bright golden signature that was me. I took note of the coordinates floating above my symbol and stuck them on an imaginary door in my mind. "I've got the coordinates and put them on a door."

"Good work, Lily. I knew you had the natural witch instinct. Now, you need to say, 'Save this landing space for me in the form of a doorway temporary.'"

I repeated her words, and the map flashed in my mind then dimmed. I had no idea if it had worked. "Done. But how do I know it worked?"

"You'll have to look with your other sight."

I reached inside for the power again and imagined throwing it in front of me. "Show me the magic." That was so basic, but it should show me what I needed. I grinned as the doorway appeared before me, as a rectangular golden outline of a door.

"Done."

"Excellent, Lily. Now get yourself over here."

"See you soon. Bye." I grabbed my bag and pulled the

coordinates from their safe little spot in my memory
—yay, brain!

Voices came from down the hallway, so I went into the
room leading off the study. I'd have to do this quickly,
because if anyone saw, they'd freak, or maybe they'd just
assume the place was haunted.

I dipped into the river of power and imagined the coordinates bright against a dark green door. "Take me where I
need to go, to the numbers on this door I show." A black
rectangular hole opened in the air in front of me. The
blackness swirled, silver flecks sparkling out of the mael-
strom every so often. I took a deep breath, my mouth
watering with fear. This was it. Would it work? I guessed I'd
soon know.

I hesitated. If I'd gotten the coordinates wrong, I could
end up anywhere. Best not to think of that now. The voices
from down the hall were louder—lucky there was a lot to
see in this castle, which must have slowed them down. I
really needed to get my crap together and take that step. *You
can do this, girl. Come on. Go.*

I shut my eyes and stepped forward. Which was stupid,
because blind, I wouldn't know when I'd gotten where I was
going, since doorways could end up being small tunnels if you
weren't very good at making them. A brief moment of disori-
entation had me opening my eyes quickly. My doorway wasn't
too bad, if I did say so myself. It was a short tunnel, and within
four steps, I was out the other side. I looked down at my feet: all
there! I grinned and looked up to the ceiling. *Thank you, universe.*

Woohoo! I'd made it to where I was supposed to go. I knew this because the décor was very government, who-cares-about-making-things-welcoming-or-comfortable style. The PIB reception room had a polished concrete floor, beige walls, and white ceiling. Little black ball cameras were attached in two ceiling corners, and six baby-poo-colour plastic chairs sat against one wall. The only door was a solid-looking white one with a strip of glass at head height. An intercom pad was attached to the wall next to the door. I used it to buzz... reception? I had no idea what they called it. Or was it just security? Who knew?

I peered out of the small window. Just outside was a hall-way. I jumped back when Angelica's face appeared on the other side. *Jeepers! Heart attack much?*

She opened the door and smiled. "Hello, Lily. Congratu-lations on getting here in one piece so soon."

"Thanks for the vote of confidence, Ma'am." Could she give me a proper compliment for a change?

"Everyone's waiting for us."

"That was quick."

"When I say jump, my agents do." She said that without arrogance—she was just stating a fact. Hopefully it wasn't a warning to me, although I wasn't an agent, so I could afford to be a bit ornery if I really wanted. Taking orders wasn't my strong suit, although I did like to help people. I just had to look at it like that, and getting Olivia back as soon as possible was all I really cared about right now.

My heart raced as I followed her to the security area where I put my backpack on the conveyer belt, then walked through the metal detector. This all brought back bad memories, but I had to remember there was no way I was going to be arrested this time. Right?

We cleared security. I'd walked the same hallways only a few weeks ago, and I recognised where we were headed: the dreaded meeting room. Nothing good had ever happened in there, at least not for me.

Angelica opened the door, and I followed her in. Today the head of the bureau wasn't there. I blew out a relieved breath. James, Beren, and William sat on the other side of the table, all chatter ending abruptly when they spied us. I sat in a chair opposite them, and Angelica sat at the head of the table, to my left.

"Hi," I said.

"Hi," was the simultaneous response from the three men.

"I'm calling this meeting to order." Angelica's firm tone was all business. "Lily, please explain exactly what happened this morning."

"Olivia picked me up about nine. We drove to Hever Castle. We'd been there for about fifteen minutes when she was snatched from the first-floor study. It's a room with twentieth-century stuff. I don't know if you need to know that, but just in case. Camilla came out of nowhere, knocked her unconscious with a spell, then left." I looked at my hands in my lap. It was intimidating to have them all staring at me across the table. It felt like the drilling I'd had last time.

"Did she say anything?" asked James.

"No, but she did give me a satisfied grin. Stupid witch."
I ground my back teeth together. She was not going to get
away with this. "What do you think she wants with Olivia?"

Angelica leaned back in her chair. "According to our
records, Ernest started working for Camilla a few weeks
before he met Olivia. We didn't think it was important
before, but now we think it might be. We haven't had time
to go over everything again since you called, but we can do
that now. After your comment the other day about him
being in love with Camilla, we thought we'd dig a little
deeper. Some of this information only came through this
morning." She waved her hand, and a small pile of stapled
paper appeared in front everyone. "This is the information
we have on Ernest—timeline, personality, contacts, work
history, arrest history, etcetera. There are about forty pages
there. I want you all to read that now, then we'll discuss
some theories."

Excuse me? Arrest history? I focussed on the first page and
started reading. He was born in London, to an investment
banker and housewife. My mouth fell open. Ernest wasn't
even his real name, and neither was the one that had been
on his airline ticket! His name was Frederick Anderson
Smythe. He went to some private schools—I say *some*,
because he went to about six different schools, which wasn't
normal for someone who'd stayed at the same address his
whole childhood. He'd been a bit of a handful—and yes,
that was the polite word for it. He'd been accused of stealing
from other students—from phones to lunch money—and
he'd even been caught on school grounds selling stolen

property, which he swore he found on the street near his house. I wondered if he'd been too young for them to do anything but give him a slap on the wrist or if his father had bribed the schools or other kids' parents.

I lifted my head. "Do we know if his father ever bribed anyone to keep things quiet about his school crimes?"

"That's on page thirteen, dear." Angelica hadn't even lifted her head from reading to answer.

I paged to thirteen. Nothing had been officially recorded by the schools, of course, but whoever had done this research had done an exceptional job. There were copies of three of the principals' bank accounts showing a lump sum of fifty-thousand pounds went into each one at dates just after the offences were mentioned in the reports, and it looked like two of the parents of wronged children had also been paid off, albeit with smaller amounts. I shook my head. How was it even legal to get this stuff? Big Brother could get anything they wanted. Scary. Although, in this instance, it was for a good cause. I supposed the principals felt like they were getting a great deal: money for nothing, and they also got to wave the kid off to a new school. I bet they'd given him good references just to get rid of him. Bastards.

His dad's income was listed here as four hundred thousand pounds a year. Holy crap! Why would Ernest, Frederick, whatever, need to steal? Attention, boredom, or because he could?

He'd gone to Arden University in Coventry and done an accounting and finance degree. While there, he was arrested twice: once for drunken disorderly behaviour, and the other

for raping a fellow female student. Wow, nice guy. His father
had bailed him out of the first charge, and the second didn't
stick after the witness withdrew her complaint and moved to
Scotland. He managed to complete his degree and went to
work in London, for his father. The whole time he'd
attended university, he'd lived at home, and his bank
account showed his dad paid him an allowance of one thousand pounds a week—lucky bastard. Once he went to work,
at a large investment bank his father worked for, he received
a salary of fifteen hundred pounds a week, which wasn't bad
for a graduate. So why had he left to work in Westerham,
which was likely less exciting and probably paid less,
unless…? Unless you could fleece old people out of their life
savings because you found a person who thought the same
way you did.

Since he'd left his job with his father, he'd moved to
Westerham, and it looked like they'd had no contact. What
the hell had happened? "We need to interview his father or
someone else at that company and find out why he left. I
have a feeling he was fired."

"You and me both, sis."

"Can someone do that while we go and find Olivia?"
The longer we sat here, the more Camilla and Ernest could
be doing to her. I bit my nail.

Angelica shook her head. "We have a different angle
now, dear. We need to cover all our bases if we don't want
this to bite us in the behind later. We'll have to interview his
father first. It's important we have Ernest's, or should I say,
Frederick's motivation for leaving. If he were fired, it would

give us a motive for what he does next. Maybe he's angry at his father and has something to prove?"

"But can't someone get onto finding where they are, at least, so we can act as soon as we have the other information?" This waiting was driving me crazy.

"Finish reading the report, and then we'll decide exactly what's going to happen." She'd already started writing a list, so she must've already decided what was going to happen. I resisted an eye roll.

My knee jiggled up and down under the table as I read the rest. Sitting here reading wasn't going to save Olivia. Now I knew what a bastard Smythe was, I didn't give a crap about saving him from Camilla. It was looking more and more like he was the instigator, not her.

I finished reading everything, just before the boys. I looked up. "Do you think Smythe set all this up and conned Camilla? I always assumed she was the mastermind because she was a witch, but her bitchy behaviour towards Olivia at the café makes sense now. She's in love with him too, like honestly in love. She was jealous of Olivia. The hate rolled off her when she was getting her morning coffee. It was almost like she was there just to torment her. It's not like she couldn't have gone to a different café if they always burnt her coffee, which was something she used to always say."

"I think we're all guilty of that assumption about the dynamics of their relationship." William looked disappointed, and I assumed it was with himself.

I felt bad for him. "It probably doesn't hurt to remember

that non-witches can be just as evil as witches. Witches don't have the monopoly on being crappy."

James smiled. "You do know you're a witch, right?"

"Oops. I forgot." Which wasn't hard to do since I'd been a non-witch for twenty-four years. Being a witch was super new to me, and I still didn't think of myself as such.

Angelica put her pen down. "If you have time for chatting, it looks like we've all finished reading?"

"Yes, Ma'am," confirmed Beren.

Angelica continued. "In light of recent information, I'm sure we can all agree that Frederick Smythe and Camilla are at least responsible for these crimes in equal parts." We all nodded. "I think she's covered her tracks and left him exposed as a blackmail chip for later. He wouldn't even realise." Wow, it was the perfect relationship. They totally deserved each other.

"Because she doesn't trust him?" I asked.

Angelica smiled. "Exactly. Camilla's a smart witch—the things she's been able to do with her magic proves it. If we found this stuff on Frederick, I have no doubt Camilla is aware of some of it too. She wouldn't have access to everything we have, but being a witch with her computer knowledge, hacking government systems wouldn't be beyond her."

"So, now what? The longer we sit around, the more danger Olivia's in."

"I was getting to that." Ma'am—not Angelica, because that was definitely Ma'am's bossy face—frowned at me. "I'm sending James and William to interview the father, because James can detect lies, and William can read minds.

They won't have to ask too many questions to get the answers they need."

Wow, they had massive advantages over non-witches. They could solve so many normal-people crimes if they wanted to that it wasn't funny. I wondered why they didn't. I guess I'd leave that question for another day. "What about me?"

"You can take Beren and me back to where your friend was taken, and we'll confirm the magic signature. Then we'll all head to Camilla's apartment, so you can take some photos. I've no doubt they won't return there. Snatching Olivia seems like a desperate move. It was done recklessly."

"Maybe they did it to taunt us? They made sure I saw. I mean, they could have taken her from her house."

"True, Lily. But I sense there's more to it."

I gave this some thought while James and William stood. "See you both later," James said. William just gave us a nod, and then they were gone.

"Be careful," I said to the empty spaces where they'd recently stood. You had to be quick around here. Sheesh. Then something hit me. "Do you think Ern—, I mean Frederick targeted Olivia on purpose, in the beginning? Her parents are really rich. Maybe he never wanted to marry her at all. Maybe he wanted to fleece her parents out of some money then run, but with our investigation closing in on them, and the wedding looming, he decided to move things forward?"

"Nice thinking." Beren beamed at me from across the table.

I blushed.

Angelica stood. "I think you definitely have a good theory there, Lily. Now we need to gather some proof, so we can charge Camilla with kidnapping as well as everything else, and hopefully find your friend before..." She let it hang, probably realising what she was about to say.

I stared at her, swallowed, and shook my head slowly. "No. We're going to get to her in time. We have to."

"Lead the way then," Angelica said.

Because I wasn't strong enough to take them with me, I let my mind-shield drop so Angelica could ferret around and get the coordinates. My shoulders tensed the whole time, but she didn't take long.

She stared at Beren. "Here."

"Thanks."

Wow, she'd just sent a message straight to his brain. My mouth hung open. What the hell?

"If you study enough, dear, you'll be able to do it too. Now come on. There's no time to waste."

I performed my spell and left the PIB behind.

CHAPTER 12

We stepped out of the doorway at Hever Castle to a woman screaming. Crap. I should have put it somewhere more private... like the toilet. Angelica swiftly put her hands on the woman's shoulders and looked into her eyes. After a few seconds, Angelica dropped her hands, and the woman shook her head... quietly.

The stranger blinked. "Oh, I just had a dizzy spell. I think I need to sit down."

Angelica adopted a sweet voice, one I never knew she possessed. "Oh, my dear. There's a chair in the next room. I'm sure they won't mind if you use it. Come with me." As she led her away, she looked back at us and gave a nod.

Beren must have known what to do, because he turned to me. "Where is the exact spot they left from?" I stood next to the window overlooking the inner courtyard and stopped.

"Here. I was standing there." I pointed across the small room.

"Okay." He put his hands on my shoulders and gently moved me a few steps away. "I need to see the magic, and your signature will get muddled into it if you're standing right there."

"Oh." You learned something new every day. Although, these days, I was learning so many new somethings that my head was spinning. He mumbled a bit and swept his hand in a circle.

Angelica's voice drifted in from the other room, probably trying to distract the woman so she didn't come back in here so soon, not that Beren seemed to be doing much, although his behaviour—staring at a spot in front of a window—may have been considered odd.

While he worked, I stepped out into the corridor to see if anyone else was coming. A couple at the other end of the hall chatted while looking at a piece of paper one of them held—probably a castle map.

"Done."

I went back into the study. "That was quick." Colour me impressed.

Angelica appeared at the other doorway. "Let's get going." She walked past us and down the stairs. I snatched my and Olivia's umbrellas out of the container and followed Angelica out the front door, across the courtyard, over the drawbridge, and towards the surrounding gardens. It was still raining, so I put my umbrella up and ran to catch Angelica.

"Here, Ma'am. You can use Olivia's umbrella."

She took it from me without stopping. "Thank you, dear."

Beren looked at me as we hurried along. "Hey, no fair!"

"Wanna share?"

"Okay."

Beren put his arm around me and took control of the umbrella, since he was taller. It was nice and cosy under there, but it was harder to walk fast squished together, and my arms and legs were getting wet because he was holding it up too high. This wasn't working out very well, at least not for me. "Can I take it back?"

"Take what back," he asked.

"My umbrella. I'm getting too wet."

"But you're keeping me warm, and I'm fairly dry."

I rolled my eyes. "But you have more umbrella than me."

He adjusted it slightly to my side. "Is that better?"

He wasn't giving up without a fight. I blew out a breath. "Yeah, whatever."

Beren grinned. "That's my girl."

His girl? I hoped he meant that in a platonic way. I did like him—I mean, who wouldn't? He was handsome, easy-going, funny, clever, nice, but...

But he wasn't William.

I couldn't help but remember the saying: If you can't be with the one you love, love the one you're with. Not that he was offering love. I was blowing things out of proportion again. I had to stop reading things into throwaway comments. We were friends, and that's all he probably meant.

A hill spread out before us, and Angelica led us off the path and behind a massive tree. She turned her head this way and that, probably checking to see we were hidden, then handed me Olivia's umbrella. She stared into my eyes. Big gold coordinates popped into my mind. "That's where we're going. Make it quick." She stepped forward and disappeared.

Beren handed me my umbrella and drew his gun. "Thanks, Lily." Then he popped away too. That's the thanks I got for keeping people dry. I sighed and awkwardly folded both umbrellas, shook them, and slid them into the side pocket of my bag. Looked like it was time to go.

I took heed that Beren had drawn his gun—things may not be totally safe on the other side—mumbled the spell, and stepped into a dry, warm apartment.

Angelica, gun in hand, was cautiously opening a door that led from the living area to who knew where. Beren stalked off in the other direction, over lime-washed timber floors. I figured I'd stay put until they'd swept the apartment. I went to one of the tall living-room windows and gazed out.

We were back in Paris. Despite the circumstances, I couldn't help a small smile. And it had been so easy. I couldn't wait to try travelling when this was all over. The places I could go, and it was free and instantaneous. Ah, travelling, where have you been all my life?

The apartment was on the second floor and overlooked

the street we'd been parked in the other day. The car crash seemed like ages ago. Beren's healing had been incredible— it was as if my body hadn't been through anything. My mind knew differently though. I'd had nightmares about it for the last two nights. I expected more of the same tonight.

Beren yelled out, "Clear!"

Angelica responded in kind. They breezed back into the room. "Okay, Lily. Let's not waste any time. See if you can find anything that will show where they went."

I scanned the room. "We may have to go downstairs again. I feel like that makes the most sense. They probably drove somewhere."

"First let me check the last time Camilla performed magic here." Angelica shut her eyes and turned in a slow circle on the spot.

I took my camera out of my bag, because I may as well make sure I didn't miss anything. "Show me any evidence of where Camilla and Frederick went when they last left here." I put the camera up to my face and roamed the apartment. There were two bedrooms. The first showed me nothing, but in the second, Camilla and Frederick sat on the double bed, fully clothed, thanks be to the gods, looking at a laptop screen. Packed suitcases waited next to the bed. I walked around to the head of the bed and focussed my lens on the laptop screen. "Nice." A villa in the French Riviera. They sure were making the most out of all the money they'd stolen. I couldn't wait to help put them in jail. I hoped Camilla got the stinkiest cell there was.

After taking a couple of photos, I finished my circuit of

the apartment and found Angelica. "Here. According to the date and time on the computer, they *have* been back here since you visited. I'm surprised there wasn't some kind of trap waiting for us."

"She may not have had enough time to set one." Angelica looked at the camera screen. "Nice."

On the screen was a gorgeous, rendered-brick two-storey villa painted yellow with white trim and terracotta-tiled roof. It was set against stunning blue water with white, barren hills across the water. Yachts were moored in the sea. The ad said Saint Jean Cap Ferrat, and there was a rental agent's number. "Yeah, that's what I said. Is Saint Jean Cap Ferrat a big place?"

"No. It's a small seaside area near Nice." *Ha, Nice, nice. Never mind.*

Beren came in. "Any leads?"

Angelica nodded. "Yes. Can you contact William, and tell him to get here as soon as the interview is over? I'm just going to use the little girl's room."

What? Wasn't she a bit old to be calling it a little girl's room? Maybe it was a British thing. Beren pulled his phone out of his pocket and pressed a couple of buttons, and I went back to the window, to take in the Parisian streets one last time. Funny how it was disgusting weather back in Britain, and here it was sunny. The plane trees stood in their verdant glory, framing the road as far as I could see.

Beren stood next to me. "Enjoying the view?"

"Yep, totally. I can't believe I didn't get to see anything properly."

"We'll come back next week. Your friend will be safely back at home, and Camilla and Fred will be in jail, giving me plenty of time to show you around the place."

As worried as I was about Olivia, there was still room for a tiny bit of excitement. "That would be beyond awesome, Beren. I'd love that."

"What would you love?" asked a new voice.

I turned around. William and James had just arrived, and William didn't look too impressed.

"Beren's going to bring me back here once this is all over. I have lots of sightseeing to do."

"Enjoy your date." William turned and left through one of the doors. That was weird.

James and Beren shared a smirk.

"What was all that about?" I asked.

Beren answered. "Oh, nothing. Poor little diddums got up on the wrong side of bed today, I'd guess."

"How'd the interview go, big bro?" I sucked at making spells rhyme, but in everyday conversation, I was awesome.

"It went well. But I'll save the explanation till Ma'am comes back."

"Well, here I am. What happened?" She came in and joined us at the window.

"I'd prefer we did this outside." James looked around and pointed to his ear. Angelica nodded.

We all filed out the front door, William coming out last. At least he was still with us, but he trailed behind, like you tend to do when you're an angry child walking behind your parents, trying to stay as far away from them as possible.

Something else I'd have to figure out later. Maybe something happened at the interview because there was no way he would be upset that Beren was bringing me back here later. Unless he was worried Beren would use me and dump me. That wasn't happening because we were friends, and James didn't seem too worried. I refused to believe it was because William was jealous. If he liked me that much, he would've asked me out by now—he'd had weeks to do that. But I knew he wouldn't. Besides, it would complicate things with James, so we were better off not acting on any attraction. Argh, I just wanted to get out of my own head. Overthinking alert!

Out on the street, stylish Parisians sauntered past. One had three dachshunds walking on leads, the dogs' little legs moving at the speed of light to keep up with their owner's fast walk. So cute! Not as cute as squirrels, but still adorable.

"So," James began. We huddled around him, which must have looked funny because they were all wearing their black PIB suits and ties. I was the nonconformist of the group. *How unusual.* "The interview went well. Smythe senior didn't want to answer anything, but once he figured out we knew everything, he spilled." James grinned.

"But you didn't know everything."

"No, Lily, but he thought we did. With William reading his mind, he asked questions he wouldn't have known to ask otherwise."

"So your truth-telling talents weren't even needed?"

"I suppose not, but anyway, Smythe senior had to fire Frederick after he was caught embezzling funds from one client. They replaced the funds before the client found out, but Smythe Junior was fired. Senior gave him a good reference anyway but cut off all ties with his son. The shame of having a criminal for a son was humiliating, so he distanced himself as far as he could, not that he was a loving father anyway. From what he said, he's always worked fourteen-to-sixteen-hour days and goes golfing or to polo with clients on the weekends. So, we're probably dealing with a damaged human who has something to prove to his father."

Made sense. Whatever the reason, it was clear now that no one should have any sympathy for that piece of crap. I hope he hadn't hurt Olivia physically. For sure she was probably wishing she were dead after finding out her fiancé was a cheating, lying thief. God, what must she think of being transported to the south coast of France without remembering how she got there? She was likely freaking out right now. I wished I could give her a hug and get her out of there.

"Can we get going?" As much as I loved Paris, Olivia needed us *now*.

"Okay, Miss Impatient." Angelica spelled open the security door to Camilla's apartment building, and we all went back inside, which was a good idea. I can't imagine what would happen if we all just disappeared off the street in front of everyone.

"I'll grab the coordinates." James pulled out his phone as he entered the building foyer. "Where are we going, Ma'am?"

"Saint Jean Cap Ferrat. As close to the centre of town as

possible." She looked up. I followed her gaze to a security camera. Her lips moved without any sound coming out. Being caught on camera was another bad idea. Lucky Angelica had everything covered.

James pulled up something on his phone and typed. When it was done loading, he gave the phone to Angelica. She nodded and passed the phone to William who looked and handed it to Beren. Beren checked it out then handed it to me. "Picture those numbers, Lily."

I looked at the screen. Coordinates were such long numbers, but if I told my brain to basically take a photo of it, maybe it would just happen rather than me having to remember each number in sequence, which would be impossible when I only had one minute to study it. I concentrated, then shut my eyes. The numbers appeared in large gold lettering, same as every other time. *Yes!*

I held the phone out without opening my eyes. "Here, James."

He laughed and took the phone. "Holding onto the number, huh?"

"Yes. I'm going to do my spell now. Wish me luck."

"You don't need luck. You've got this." Beren was so sweet. If only I was as attracted to him as I was to stupid William.

I whispered, "Take me where I need to go, to the numbers on this door I show." When I opened my eyes, my doorway was right where it should be. I just hoped it was going to lead to the right place.

South of France, here I come!

CHAPTER 13

The landing place was a toilet cubicle just like any other. I didn't waste time, because Angelica was about to come through her door, and I was in her way. I opened the cubicle door and stepped out. One of the other stalls looked occupied, but the hand-washing area was empty. As soon as Angelica opened the cubicle door, I went through the main door, which led into a separate attendant's area.

A short, rotund older lady wearing a blue apron over her clothes stood there staring at me, her eyes wide. They had toilet attendants? Oh dear. She might need some memory tampering, because two women whom she had never seen go in just exited. Angelica swept past me and straight to the lady whose mouth was hanging open in silent surprise. Poor thing.

Angelica placed her hands on the woman's cheeks and

looked into her eyes. After a minute, she dropped her hands and smiled at the woman. "Au revoir."

The woman smiled through her confused expression, and Angelica practically pushed me out the door. A hallway led to another door. Angelica opened it, and we stepped out into the street. The guys were waiting outside in the sunshine, and they'd changed clothes. Gone were the sexy black suits and ties, and in their place were T-shirts and board shorts. They were wearing running shoes rather than thongs. Of course, William had to have nice legs. Long with lean muscle. Nice calves. I looked up. He'd caught me checking him out. He smirked, and I blushed.

I quickly turned to James. "Blending in, I see?"

"Don't you know it." My brother looked like he'd been working out. His arms had never been that big back home. I guessed his job demanded it. When we were younger and went to the beach, he was always the skinny kid, with stick-thin arms. That memory made me think of my mum, who used to take us to the beach all the time in summer. God, I missed her.

A family with three kids walked past, all carrying boogie boards and dressed in beach gear. It wasn't that warm at twenty-two degrees. Crazy Europeans, but at least they were having fun. *Enjoy it while you can.* I hoped they'd get many happy years together.

Angelica was still in her suit, but I supposed someone had to be the sensible adult. "I'm going to have a chat to the real estate rental company for that house. I'll be back in a moment." She turned and went into the door next to the one we'd just come out of. Talk about convenient.

The narrow street was one-way. Palm trees lined the footpath, and the buildings were two, three, or four stories with signs proclaiming Holiday Apartments everywhere. The buildings were rendered and painted pastel colours, and most windows had pretty timber shutters. A familiar salty tang hung in the air. I wandered past the real estate agent, which was on the street corner, and stopped dead. *Would you look at that!*

Framed by small mountains on one side, a turquoise bay stretched into the distance. A mess of yacht masts and rigging rose towards the cerulean sky, and in the marina, motorboats waited to be used by their rich owners. This was truly the playground of the rich. The boats were all huge with lots of windows and more than one storey. Ah, to be loaded and cruise around in the sun all day eating smoked salmon and chocolate mousse. The boat owners probably had chefs, personal shoppers, and someone to do their grocery shopping too. Bastards. And this was the life stupid Camilla and Frederick were after. By the time we'd finished with them, they *would* have someone cooking their meals and buying their clothes, but not the way they expected.

I breathed in the sea air. Where was the house? Could I see it from here? The Internet listing showed it was on a hill overlooking the water. I said quietly, "We're coming, Liv. Hang on."

Shoes clopped on the concrete. "There you are."

Angelica stopped next to me. "I have the address. I just need to clear with you what's going to happen, so you know."

"Okay." I turned to face her.

"We're going to get a taxi to the house, which is about a three-minute drive that way." She pointed to the right, to one side of the bay. "I want you to stay hidden. I don't think Camilla will attack us, but we can't be sure, and we're not underestimating Frederick. He could have a weapon, and we don't want him hurting Olivia. So you're to stay out of the way until I tell you. When I give the word, you're to race in and grab Olivia. Not one moment before. Understood?"

"Understood." I may have bent the rules when it was just my own safety, but I wouldn't compromise my friend's.

"And don't use any magic until we're engaged—not that you should need to, since you're staying out of sight. If we use any magic, they'll know we're there."

"Okay."

"Taxi's here," Beren called out from the corner.

When I reached the kerb, James shook his head. "You'll have to wait here with William. The taxi can only take four at the most, and I won't leave you by yourself. We'll scope the place out while the taxi comes back for you two." He clapped William on the back and slid into the car.

William still had the scowl on his face when he turned around.

"Well, aren't you just a happy agent today. Surely you can muster up a smile for our gorgeous locale."

He kept his scowl on me for a few more seconds then

stalked off to stare out at the water. Well, apparently I was wrong. There would be no smile-mustering today.

While I waited for the taxi to return, I checked out the listings in the real estate agent's window. I nearly choked at the prices. Six-bedroom villa to rent. Sleeps twelve. Twenty thousand euros per week. The pictures were stunning, and so was the view over the water from the place, but not at that price.

After checking out the rest of the unattainable gorgeousness, I kept an eye out for the taxi. When it finally returned, I called Agent Crankypants over. I was already in the taxi and buckled up by the time he reached us.

The taxi drove through the town centre and took a street that climbed a hill. Some of the homes were hidden by tall walls, but some were perched high enough that I could see them. If you were into mansions, this would be the place for you. "Wow, look at that!" The view of the water out of William's side of the car took my breath away.

"Yeah, it's nice, but we need to focus, Lily."

"Okay."

He was right. I was so easily distracted, but could he blame me? It wasn't my fault the criminals they were chasing just happened to come to one of the most beautiful places on earth.

The taxi pulled over, although the road was so narrow, there wasn't any room to stay parked. I slid out, and William paid with what I assumed was a PIB credit card.

The property was on the low side of the street. Metal gates hung from impressive brick pillars. The only thing visible of the property was the driveway that wound down the hill until it got lost in greenery. The shimmering sea did its thing in the background to dazzle me. But then I remembered Olivia down there, probably suffering. How were we going to get over those gates? Not to mention, there was a security camera on a pole two metres inside the gates. "How do we get in?"

"Angelica's turned off the security system. I'll help you onto the top of the brick fence, and you can climb down the other side. It won't be hard. Just hang onto the top of the wall and walk your legs down, then drop. It's not far." Easy for him to say when he was so much taller than me.

We approached the wall, and he knelt. "Climb on."

What? "Where?"

"My shoulders."

I eyed him sceptically. "Look, no offence, but will you be able to lift me. I'm not that light you know."

He raised his brow. "Trust me. You're small fry. And if I do have trouble, I can always call on my magic."

"No, you can't. Angelica said not to."

"Yeah, yeah, I know. Have a little trust, Lily. I won't hurt you. I promise."

Without reading anything deeper into his comment, I climbed on. I clutched his head. Ooh, his hair was so soft. "Sorry. There's nothing else to hold onto."

He slowly stood, and I wobbled and gripped his head harder.

"Ow. Can you not crush my skull?"

"I don't want to fall."

He walked to the wall. "Hold onto the wall, and then I'll help you stand on my shoulders."

"Are you kidding? Actually, scratch that. You never kid." Or smile, or laugh, or have fun.

"I take offence to that."

"You can't be serious."

"I kid all the time. Just not in front of you."

"Well, it's nice to know you save your crappiest self for me. I really appreciate the effort."

"Are you going to climb the wall, or should I just leave you out here?"

Argh. How did I like this man? He made me so mad. "Grrr. Fine."

"Did you just growl at me?"

"Maybe." I gripped the rough bricks. "I'm going to stand. Don't drop me."

"Haven't we been through this?"

I carefully lifted one foot. William helped by pushing it up and holding onto my shin. I wobbled, almost falling backwards. My fingers dug into the wall harder. Crap. This was never going to work. My heart raced as I leaned forward and prepared to lift my other foot into place. I pushed down on the foot that was on his shoulder, straightening my leg and standing while leaning harder against the wall. He trembled as my other foot landed on his shoulder. Adrenaline shot through my stomach. He gripped the calf of my other leg, so he was steadying both my legs. And we were still upright. Thank God.

I walked my fingers up to the top of the wall. "I'm holding the top of the wall."

"Okay. I'm going to put my hands under your shoes and hoist you up. And that's it."

Ah huh. That's it. As easy as doing a backflip off a moving horse. Okay, so it was easier, but still…. My fingers ached as I made claws of steel. Nothing would make me let go now. I teetered as his palms lifted slightly so that I was standing on them.

"Ready, set. Go!" He lifted, and I pulled. But he'd pushed so hard that my body didn't stop when my legs reached the top. They flew over, and my toes slammed into the wall on the other side as I hung on for dear life. Jesus. That was not supposed to happen. I looked down. It was only about five feet to the ground from the end of my shoes, so I let go and dropped to a crouch.

William gracefully flew over the wall and landed next to me. He straightened and put his hands on his hips. "See. I didn't drop you."

"Yes, but you threw me over the wall. I wasn't expecting it. Have a little consideration." I brushed my hands down my jeans to get the brick grit off them. They stung from being scraped, but whatever. I'd worry about that later. "So, what now?"

"Let's make our way to the house. Quietly, and I'll lead." William pulled out his handgun.

And things just got real.

We crept through expensive landscaping, keeping low and behind shrubbery as much as possible. 007 came to mind. The only things I was missing was a gun and an evening dress, oh and the stilettos, because all good movie heroines have to save the world in ridiculously inappropriate footwear.

As we snuck down the hill, the two-storey mansion came into view bit by bit. The terracotta-tiled roof was bright against the blue sea. The smooth, rendered walls were painted a soft yellow. Large timber windows with shutters all painted white gave the place a beachy, happy feel, but what was about to go down would not be in the least cheery.

James crouched under one ground-floor window, to the left of the front door, and Beren and Angelica stood on either side of the entry, guns ready. We were about twenty metres from the house. I grabbed William's arm to stop him. I made sure to whisper. "Should I hide here somewhere? I don't want to get caught in the middle of a gun fight."

"Good idea. Angelica will send you a mind message when she needs you."

"Straight into my head?"

"Yes."

"Will I hear it, or will it be in word pictures, like the coordinates?"

"You'll hear her voice."

"That's cool."

"Yes, it is. Stay safe, Lily."

"I will. You too." He kept eye contact for a second more than was necessary, sending warmth through my body all the way to my toes. Damn him. And then he was crouch running to where James hid. Once he reached James, he lay on the ground and crawled to the left of James and to the corner of the house. He disappeared around the corner, heading for the back of the house. *Please don't get hurt.*

I sat behind a large tree fern and poked my head just far enough out to see Angelica and Beren. Angelica nodded to Beren, put her hand on the doorknob, then pushed the door open. She pivoted back and let Beren run in first, his gun raised in front of him. She ran in after. James stood, looked in the window, then ran for the front door too.

My heart pounded. I held my breath and listened for shouting or gunshots. My gaze darted from the front door to the corner where William had disappeared and back again. I was going to have a heart attack just waiting for this to go down.

Was Olivia still alive? I swallowed. Crap. If I let myself go there, I'd end up in the foetal position on the ground.

A seagull cawed directly above as it glided to the water. I started, my heart pummelling my ribs. *Jesus. Give a witch a break.* I tried to slow my breathing and listened. Muffled shouts from inside the house disturbed the refined silence of the wealthy enclave. Oh my God. Was everyone okay? What was happening? I swallowed again, my mouth working overtime on the saliva.

More shouting, this time coming from the back of the house. Should I investigate? Did they need me? I knelt, getting ready, just in case. *Come on, Angelica. Call me, dammit.*

A low rumble came from the far side of the yard, down the hill and to my right. The ground also rose from where I hid to the driveway, the land having a cross fall towards me and to the water. A black car sped past up the driveway. Crap. I jumped up. *Was Olivia in there?*

I screamed out for Angelica as I ran up the hill, chasing the car as it headed for the main gates. They would get away over my dead body. I didn't climb that damn wall for nothing.

I sprinted faster, James calling out my name from behind me, but I couldn't stop. I wasn't going to let them escape. The large iron gates had started to open, and I was still thirty metres from the car. My breathing was ragged, and my legs burned as I pushed harder. I stooped to pick up a large rock as I ran. It was just bigger than my hand, and I was going to use it to smash their windows.

The gates were almost open enough for the car to get through, and I was close enough to see Frederick at the wheel. The engine revved. *No!* They were going to get away.

Then the gates stopped opening, a couple of centimetres shy of being big enough for the car to get through. It must've been someone's magic. The hair on my nape stood on end. Someone else was casting a spell. Was it us or them?

I reached the passenger window, but Camilla wasn't there. Dark tinting covered the back windows, and I put my face up to them and looked in.

Camilla sat in the back with a tied-up, gagged, and pissed-off looking Olivia. I let out a rush of breath. Thank God she was still alive. I tried to open the back door, but it was locked. Camilla's mouth was moving. That wasn't a good sign.

It was like thousands of ants were climbing all over my head, and the gates started opening.

I reached my arm back and slammed the rock against the front passenger window. Glass smashed. The engine revved. With tyres squealing, the car burst out of the front entry.

James ran past me and thrust his hands out.

Instead of turning onto the road, the car drove straight and crashed into a high brick fence on the opposite side of the street. Yay, James! He ran to the driver side of the car. I followed but stayed on the passenger side, figuring we needed to cover all exits.

Camilla was already getting out of the back, dragging Olivia with her. Was she going to take her through a doorway again? Panting came from behind me. I turned. Beren pointed his gun at Camilla and yelled, "Stop!"

She grinned like a maniac and stepped forward, one foot disappearing into a doorway I couldn't see. A huge crack split the air as Beren pulled the trigger. The bullet hit Camilla in the shoulder. She dropped Olivia and fell backwards, her foot reappearing as she hit the ground. Beren ran and tackled her, cuffing her with what I assumed were the anti-magic cuffs. He didn't muck around.

James was on the driver side trying to pull the door open. Frederick, inside, held it shut. At least he couldn't lock the car now one of the doors was open. What an idiot. It wasn't like he could go anywhere. He should just give up.

I wrenched open the front passenger door—it was a bit stiff because the panels were slightly out of whack after the crash—the screech of complaining metal hurting my ears almost as much as the gunshot.

Still holding his door with one hand, Frederick glared at me, his cheeks red, eyes ablaze. He was way angry.

Well, bad luck, Donald Duck. Today is not going to be your day.

He screamed, frothing at the mouth. "I had this all set up, and you came along… you and your stupid PIB chaps. Why do you think I chose Olivia?" His yell turned into a manic laugh. "Her father is rich, and I was this close"—he held his thumb and pointer finger a centimetre apart—"to acquiring some of that for myself. Don't think I'm going away without retribution." He reached under his seat, pulled out a gun, and pointed it at me.

My eyes widened. "He's got a gun!" My stomach dropped, and I sucked in a breath of air.

"I'm not going down alone," he said, the crazy glint in his eyes slicing right through me.

I stumbled backwards, but I was too slow. Another shot exploded, pretty much obliterating my eardrums, pain lancing through my ears. Blood splattered over the cream-leather seat and my clothes. My life flashed in front of my eyes—my parents, my photography, how James would deal with this, Angelica, and Beren, regret at not ever getting to kiss William. Argh, I'd turned into a sap on my deathbed, when I should be embracing the panic. Tears burned my eyes, and I looked down, expecting to see blood spurting out of my stomach.

Frederick gurgled. My head snapped up. Blood bubbled up through his mouth and fountained down his chin. The gun fell from his hand, and he slumped towards me, his head landing on the passenger seat with a tiny thud.

My legs gave way, and my butt slammed into the ground. What the hell had just happened? I blinked and stared sightlessly at the top of Frederick's head.

"Lily!" James must have run around the car, because all of a sudden he was on the ground next to me, his hand on my chin, lifting my face. "Are you hurt? Are you okay? Answer me!"

His voice was faint over the ringing in my ears. "I— I'm fine. I think." Was I yelling? I patted myself down and nodded, my breath coming fast. I wasn't going to die. Sweet baby Jesus. "Yes, I'm fine. Olivia. How's Olivia?"

"I think she's okay but in shock. Beren's untying her now, and Ma'am's transporting Camilla to PIB headquarters. Jesus, Lily, I thought he was going to kill you." James dragged his palm down his face. "What happened to staying out of it?"

"But they were getting away. I couldn't let them. I just couldn't. I didn't mean to get involved. It's like my brain has a mind of its own. It just wanted to save Olivia."

James snorted. "Your brain has a mind of its own. Now I've heard everything." He squeezed me in a hug. "Thank God you're okay. Don't ever scare me like that again."

"I'm sorry. I'll try not to." My voice was muffled against his shirt.

"I suppose that's the best you're going to give me."

"What's going to happen to Olivia? Are you going to wipe her memory?"

"We'll need a statement first."

William's voice floated from above. "Lily? There's someone here who wants to see you."

James released me. I looked up. Olivia stood there with Beren and William behind her. Her cheek was bruised, hair messy, and she had her arms wrapped around her middle. Her eyes glistened. She looked like a person defeated.

"Olivia!" I jumped up and squished her in the biggest hug ever. Looked like circumstance was slowly beating my hug aversion out of me.

She hugged me back and cried. "God, am I glad to see you. I—I don't know what happened. He didn't love me, Lily. Everything was a sham." She shook with sobs.

"Hey, it's going to be okay." I held her tighter. "I'm so sorry he was a fraud, but you're going to get through this. You really are, and I'll be with you every step of the way. I'm so sorry I couldn't tell you anything. I hope you don't hate me."

She hiccupped. "Of course not. You didn't make him do all those evil things. But I'm sad and angry, confused. I hate him, yet I still love him. How is that possible?"

"You don't have to process it all now. Everything you're feeling is normal. Just go with it, and we'll take it day by day. Okay?"

She nodded. Beren put his hand on her shoulder. "Time to go. I'm going to transport you to PIB headquarters, as we need to ask you some questions. Are you okay with that, Olivia?"

She stepped back from me and nodded again.

"I'll see you soon, Liv, okay?"

She looked at me, her face overflowing with sadness. She gave a small wave as Beren put his arm around her and guided her through a doorway.

"Lily?" James was using his I-need-you-to-do-me-a-favour voice.

"What do you need me to do?" I didn't have the energy to make him work for it.

"Can you take photos of the scene? We need them for forensics, plus can you can get a photo of the moment he pulled the gun on you? We'll also have to get you to take some shots inside, see if you can get some of when they had Olivia here. It will help in court."

I looked at the ground for a moment, summoning my strength. He wanted me to relive the horror of everything right now? *But it's for the greater good. Dig deep, Lily. You didn't go through all this to have Camilla get off on a technicality, or to see James get suspended or fired for killing Frederick.*

William stepped up and put his palm on my shoulder. The heat of his hand through my top was comforting, and I leaned into him a little. "We know it's a lot to ask, but we wouldn't if we didn't have to. You know that, right?"

"Yeah, I know. I'll do it."

"We'll be here with you, Lily. And if you need to stop and take a break at any time, you can."

"Thanks." I'd had my small knapsack on my back the entire time, so I slid it off and grabbed my camera out of it. I took photos of the car from all angles, then took pics of Frederick. I gagged a couple of times and had to stop to get some fresh air, but before long, I was done. Then I stood where I'd been when he was pointing the gun at me. It took a few tries, but finally, I managed to conjure the moment he pointed the gun at me. I shuddered, my heart racing again, and had to remind myself that this wasn't real, at least not in this moment.

James and William had donned gloves and were searching the car. William bagged the gun and a pile of cash he found in the glove box.

Just before we left to examine the house, two witches, one woman and one man, stepped out of nowhere. They both wore white smocks, rubber gloves, and one carried a body bag. The one carrying the bag greeted us with a nod. "I'm Agent Michaels. We're here to examine the body and take it away." He looked through the open front passenger door. "Which one of you shot him?"

"I did." James put up his hand.

"I'll have some questions for you. Think you can stay while we do this?"

"Yeah, sure." James turned to William and me. "You guys go get started. I'll be in soon."

"Not a problem." William turned to me. "Come on. Let's get this done."

I gripped my camera and followed him down to the house. I'd be more than glad to see the end of today.

I shoulder-bumped William as we walked. "You owe me about a gazillion coffees."

"Me? What did I do?"

"Nothing much, but I have to take this out on someone, and you're it."

"I can handle anything you throw at me. I've got your back, kiddo."

"Kiddo? I'm not much younger than you. How old are you, by the way?"

"Twenty-seven."

"Okay, I suppose you are an old man."

He gasped in mock horror and covered his heart with one hand over the other. "How you wound me."

"I'm sure it would take a lot more to wound you, tough guy."

His smile fell. "It would, but never again." He quickened his stride and left me trailing behind as he entered the house. *Huh?*

I stumbled, but quickly righted myself. Okay, that was a random freak out I hadn't seen coming. I hadn't meant to hurt his feelings. *Idiot, Lily.* That chick, whoever she was, must have done a real number on him. It still surprised me that anyone would hurt him—he was the hottest guy I'd ever met, apart from the cranky disposition. Surely he would do the breaking of hearts, not the other way around?

I just wanted to run in there and give him a hug, but there was as much chance of that as of Angelica not wiping Olivia's memory of all this. How did I manage to stuff things up every single time? It must be a gift.

I pushed away the thought that William and I would never get close and raised my camera. It was time to get back to work.

CHAPTER 14

L ater that night, I gave Angelica my memory card, which had enough evidence to put Camilla away for the rest of her life. Then I lingered in a hot shower before going to bed, exhausted.

The next morning, I dragged my sorry arse out of bed and got dressed, ready for another meeting at the PIB. I went down to the kitchen and felt all the sad feels while making my coffee with the machine William had given me. As the milk frothed, I heavy sighed.

"You've hardly gotten out of bed and already the world is on your shoulders?" Angelica strode in and magicked a cup of tea into her hands. I had so much catching up to do.

"I'm just tired." I checked my mind shield was up. *Yes. Phew.*

"There's nothing you'd like to talk about?"

"No, thanks. Actually, I do have one question about yesterday. Why didn't James freeze Frederick rather than shoot him?" It had bothered me all night. I hated the guy, but did he have to die, and did I have to see his blood everywhere? You could wash that stuff out of clothes, but you couldn't wash it from your memory, although...

She ran her hand over her bun. "He can't do a freezing spell. I could have, or Beren or William, but none of us could see him properly. You need a clear line of sight, or someone else might be affected instead, and then you do more harm than good. Yesterday, he did what he was trained to do in that situation—shoot first and ask questions later. From what he tells me, there really was no time. And I agree. Would you rather he let you get shot and die?"

I refrained from rolling my eyes. "Um, no, of course not. I just wondered—that's all. And speaking of getting shot and dying, is it possible you could wipe my memory of seeing Frederick with blood everywhere? I'd prefer not to have that in my repertoire of thoughts." And who could blame me?

"I'm afraid not, dear. You need these memories for your subconscious to use later. Every experience we have is filed away by the brain so it can make more informed decisions later. When you trust your gut, it's your subconscious brain you're trusting. It gathers the most minute data you don't even know it's collecting, and next time it's in a similar situation, it compares notes with itself, and if it notices a deviation from the norm or can relate it to a similar dangerous situation, it will tell you to act."

"Huh. Interesting. That doesn't really help me though. I woke from three separate nightmares last night. I'm tired."

"You'll just have to deal with it, dear. Your generation lacks resilience."

Resilience shmilience. I sighed again and dropped my head, my energy draining through my body, down my legs, and into the floor. I wanted to go back to bed.

"Time to get a move on. Finish your coffee, and let's get going." Angelica turned and stepped through her portal.

I swallowed my coffee in five huge gulps. *So much for enjoying my favourite beverage.* Today really was starting out crap. I put my cup on the table, created my own portal, and shuffled through.

Angelica held the PIB reception room door open for me.

"Thanks for waiting." I slipped through and walked the familiar route to the conference room. I wondered if there'd been arguments with other PIB staff because she and her team were always hogging it?

I also wondered how Olivia was and how I was supposed to deal with pretending yesterday never happened. I'd call her as soon as I finished here. Ma'am opened the door for me—funny how I thought of her more as Ma'am at work and Angelica at home. I supposed it was safer that way, as I wouldn't slip up and call her the wrong thing in front of her colleagues.

I'd barely made it two steps into the room when I stopped. "Olivia?" What was she doing here? She sat between Beren and Millicent on the other side of the table.

Dark circles ringed the underside of her red eyes, but she managed a wan smile.

James sat at the base of the table, next to Millicent, and waved. William had his back to me, and being the *polite* person he was, he hadn't even turned to acknowledge I was there. We were playing it like that today, were we?

Angelica smiled as she took her place at the head of the table. "Olivia has decided not to have her mind wiped. Instead, she's going to take the non-disclosure oath."

What! I had trouble finding my voice for a moment. I was happy I could share the truth about myself with her, but what if she accidentally told someone? "But how? Why? Are you sure, Liv? That's a big decision, and you've just had so much happen." I took a seat opposite her, next to Agent Crankypants. Bad luck if he didn't like it. A heady scent tickled my nose. Why did he have to smell so good? The bad luck was clearly on me.

She sighed. "I know. The last twenty-four hours have been… trying, but I've been thinking. After going through everything, I don't want this to happen to other people. After chatting with Angelica, Millicent, and Beren,"—she spared a glance and smile for Beren. *Interesting*—"I've decided to undertake police training then become a liaison between the local police and the PIB, but I'd work for the PIB and undertake research mostly, which is what I'm good at, and I love. Millicent's going to train me and be my boss."

Millicent smiled, and she was definitely glowing. Even though the baby had given her morning sickness, her skin was clear and her eyes bright. "I sure am. I'm off dangerous fieldwork until after the baby comes, so my workload will practically halve. A witch's magic is a lot weaker than normal when they're pregnant. So it's a win-win situation."

Olivia gave her a small smile, then turned to me again. "Angelica's even mentioned there's a special project you and James are working on that I could help with, but she didn't give me the details."

Was the special project my parents' disappearance? "I still think it's a big decision to make so quickly. I just don't want you to regret it later. It's not always safe." And didn't I know that firsthand. If anything happened to her, I'd blame myself.

"I'm a big girl, Lily. If we decide it's not working out, Angelica can wipe my mind, and that's that."

I sat up straight and grinned. It had taken me a while, but I had the perfect solution. "Actually, I know something that will help... with the agreement and not accidentally dying from telling someone about witches."

"You do?" Angelica leaned forward.

"The other day, before we went to the castle, I didn't want to accidentally say something about Frederick... Ernest, so I came up with a spell, and it actually worked. I tried to say something about Ernest lying to you, but my mouth wouldn't say anything. The spell is: filter my thoughts, and only let words form for the ones that won't cause remorse. I'm sure we can just change it to suit your circumstances, but I think it's a spell that has to be renewed, like the thought-protection one."

Angelica sat back. "And you impress us, yet again. Good

work, dear. I'll let you come up with something, and we can test it." She tapped her fingers on the table. "Make a spell that encompasses all non-witches, and then we can test it on a non-witch who works here. If it works, I'll have our people come up with something that lasts longer or can last until the spell is revoked by the caster. I'd hate for Olivia to get used to the fact that she doesn't have to worry. Then, when it runs out, she's not guarding against saying those things for herself. Until we can prolong it, I wouldn't rely on it too much."

I couldn't help but smile at her praise—she didn't dole it out often. I turned to Olivia. "So, does that mean you won't be working at Costa anymore? And what are you going to tell your parents?"

"I'll have to quit Costa, but that doesn't mean we can't grab coffee there, and, at Ma'am's suggestion, I'm going to move in with you guys soon—less chance of my parents wondering what my job actually is. I'll stay with my parents for a week or two, while I process what happened." She paused and wiped a tear from her eye. I resisted the urge to jump across the table and give her a huge hug. Frederick was a total pig, but she loved him, and he'd been killed. The whole situation was almost unbelievable. "Then I'm going to tell them about the police training, and then when that's done and I start working here, I'll tell them I'm in research for a secret government department."

"Oh my God! Are you kidding? You're going to move in with us!" I squeed and happy danced in my chair, my feet bouncing up and down off the floor in joy.

William put his hands over his ears and gave me a "grow up" look. I grinned and poked my tongue out at him. He shook his head, but he wore the ghost of a smile, then looked away.

I was still grinning. "This is the best news ever!"

Angelica smiled. "I'm so glad you approve, dear. Now, we have a few things to discuss before we can close this part of the case and leave it to our legal department."

We got down to boring stuff after that, and I had to ignore the musky, jasmine scent of the cranky yet warm man next to me. I really was a sucker for punishment.

After four hours of torture, I had one last question. "Ma'am, did you get any information on the man who tried to take me?" I swallowed the torrent of nerves making my mouth water.

"Yes and no. He had his wallet on him. His licence says his name is Vlad X, but that isn't likely his real name. The license was issued in Romania five years ago. We dug deeper but couldn't find any other information on him. His magic signature was unreadable, since he was dead, and his name doesn't come up on any databases. His fingertips melted at the time of the crash too, so there was no way to run his fingerprints through the system. The autopsy shows he was badly injured in the car crash, however, he most probably died from the brain-blast spell that activated after the crash."

I blinked. "Melted fingertips? Brain-blast spell?" That sounded painful.

"The fingertips one is a spell we hadn't seen before, but

it was effective. The brain-blast spell is a small explosion that uses the brain's own electricity to fry it. Whoever he was working for wanted no loose ends, obviously."

"So we're really no closer to finding out who he works for than before?"

Ma'am pursed her lips, then answered. "I'm afraid not, Lily, but we'll keep working on it. I promise." Her gaze softened with either apology or sympathy. Either one showed she cared but also confirmed how dangerous my family's enemy was.

I wiped my clammy hands on my jeans. Would I always be a target?

Angelica stood. "Thanks for coming, everyone. Since there are no more questions, this meeting is over. Lily, would you please take Olivia home and show her around? I think the bedroom next to yours will be good. Then you can help her move her things in the next couple of weeks."

I smiled and stood. At least there was some good news to come out of today. "Yes, Ma'am."

Olivia came around to my side of the table, and I gave her a hug.

At least I had another friend that would make living this witch life a bit more fun, but that little voice in my gut warned it was just one more person to worry about. I had no doubt that whoever was after me wouldn't hesitate to hurt or use my friends to get to me. I'd just have to plan for the worst. Boy, did I have a lot of work ahead.

"Are you ready?" I asked.

"You bet." Her smile was tentative, but I was just happy it was there. Her cheeks rosy, she held out her hand.

I took it, and we stepped through my doorway and went home.

ALSO BY DIONNE LISTER

PARANORMAL INVESTIGATION BUREAU

Witchnapped in Westerham #1

THE CIRCLE OF TALIA EPIC FANTASY SERIES

Shadows of the Realm
A Time of Darkness
Realm of Blood and Fire

THE ROSE OF NERINE EPIC FANTASY SERIES

(Epic Fantasy)

Tempering the Rose

ABOUT THE AUTHOR

USA Today bestselling author, Dionne Lister is a Sydneysider with a degree in creative writing, two Siamese cats, and is a member of the Science Fiction and Fantasy Writers of America. Daydreaming has always been her passion, so writing was a natural progression from staring out the window in primary school, and being an author was a dream she held since childhood.

Unfortunately, writing was only a hobby while Dionne worked as a property valuer in Sydney, until her mid-thirties when she returned to study and completed her creative writing degree. Since then, she has indulged her passion for writing while raising two children with her husband. Her books have attracted praise from Apple iBooks and have reached #1 on Amazon and iBooks charts worldwide, frequently occupying top 100 lists in fantasy. She's excited to add cozy mystery to the list of genres she writes. Magic and danger are always a heady combination.

ACKNOWLEDGEMENTS

To Becky at Hot Tree Editing—thanks again for your wonderful insight. To Ciara and MJ for helping me name my book baby. And to my hubby, who is patiently handling my long work hours and crazy mood swings—one minute there's excitement for a new book release, then next stress from trying to meet deadlines. To Rob, my cover artist, you've made Lily come to life yet again, and I love her a little bit more every time I see her in a new piece of artwork.

Made in the USA
Monee, IL
04 February 2021